GREAT ILLUSTRATED CLASSICS

W9-ARN-366

LITTLE WOMEN
Louisa May Alcott

HEIDI
Johanna Spyri

ANNE OF GREEN GABLES
L.M. Montgomery

Published by Playmore, Inc., and Waldman Publishing Corp.,
New York, New York

GREAT ILLUSTRATED CLASSICS

Series Publisher
Anne Waldman Gober

Series Editor
Rochelle Larkin

Associate Editor
Tara Knight

Printed in Canada

LITTLE WOMEN
Louisa May Alcott

CONTENTS

About the Author

Louisa May Alcott was born in 1832, the second daughter of four. Her father, A. Bronson Alcott, was an idealistic educator and philosopher. She spent most of her life in Boston and nearby Concord, Massachusetts.

Seeing how hard her mother had to work, Louisa resolved early to make life easier for her. She took various jobs—seamstress, companion, governess and teacher—to support the family. But it was at her writing table that she was most successful. While she was in her twenties, a variety of thrillers, poems, potboilers and "sensation stories" poured forth from her pen under other names.

In 1868, her Boston publisher suggested that she write a novel for girls using scenes and people familiar to her. So, with her family's encouragement, she wrote *Little Women,* which originally appeared in two volumes.

She was able to write the book very quickly—for she had prepared for thirty-five years, and her cast of characters was her own family!

The story was an immediate and huge success. The publisher could not print copies fast enough to keep the orders filled. The demand for more of Louisa's stories was so great that she followed up with a book nearly every year till the end of her life. Among them are *Little Men, Eight Cousins, Jo's Boys* and *Under the Lilacs.*

Louisa was a great champion of causes, such as better working conditions for women and women's suffrage. She was the first woman in Concord to register to vote.

Louisa became very famous, and though life was comfortable, she felt her freedom restricted because of her fame. Her success brought her little happiness, and she died, nervous and exhausted, at the age of fifty-six.

The March Sisters

Chapter 1
Four Sisters

The four March sisters sat around the fire knitting while they waited for their mother to come home.

"Christmas won't be Christmas without any presents," grumbled Jo.

"It's so dreadful to be poor," sighed Meg.

"Some girls have all the pretty things, while others have nothing," sniffed Amy.

"But we've got Mother and Father and each other," said Beth from her corner.

"But we haven't got Father. We shall not have him for a long time," said Jo. Father was off where the fighting was. Though too old to fight, he had gone as a chaplain.

Each girl had a dollar to spend on something she wanted for Christmas. But there were to be no presents this year. Mother thought they should not spend money on pleasure when the men were suffering in the dreadful American Civil War.

Although they were poor, they were a happy and close family. The room in which they sat was comfortable and warm, though the furniture was plain.

Margaret, or Meg, was the oldest of the four at sixteen. She was pretty, with soft brown hair. Fifteen-year-old Jo was tall and thin, and something of a tomboy. Her one beauty was her long, thick hair. Beth, who was thirteen, was very shy. She had a timid voice, and she seldom left the house. Amy, though the youngest, felt herself to be very important. She had big blue eyes and curly

Father Is a Chaplain.

golden hair.

The clock struck six and reminded them that Marmee, as they called their mother, would soon be home. Suddenly they all had the same idea. They would each buy something for Marmee with their dollars.

"We must go shopping tomorrow, Meg," said Jo, marching up and down. They were all excitedly planning when Marmee, a tall, motherly lady opened the door. She was not elegantly dressed, but they thought her noble-looking. The girls helped her get her wet things off and get settled by the fire.

"I've got a treat for you after supper," said Mrs. March. "A letter from Father! A nice long letter. He is well and sends loving wishes for Christmas."

"Oh, when will he come home, Mother?" asked Beth with a quiver in her voice.

"Not for many months, unless he is sick. He will stay and do his work," said Mrs.

Getting Marmee Settled

March sadly.

They all drew to the fire to hear the letter. It was cheerful and full of news, but everyone sniffed when they came to the end. Father said he would not be back for a year. Everyone was quiet, and then they again fell to their work.

At nine they stopped work and sang before they went to bed. Beth, the musical one, played the old piano. Meg and Marmee led the singing while Jo gave a croak or two in the wrong place, and Amy chirped like a cricket. Then they all went up to bed.

The Evening Sing

"Where Is Mother?"

Chapter 2
A Merry Christmas

Jo was the first to wake on Christmas morning. No stockings hung at the fireplace. But she reached under her pillow and found a small crimson-covered book. She woke Meg, who received a green-covered book. The two younger girls each received books too.

"Where is Mother?" asked Meg as she and Jo ran downstairs. Hannah, the servant who had been with the family since Meg was born, answered that a boy had come begging and Mrs. March had gone with him to see what his family needed.

"She'll be back soon, so let's have everything ready," said Meg. The gifts were collected in a basket and put under the sofa. There were new slippers from Jo, gloves from Meg, embroidered handkerchiefs from Beth, and a bottle of perfume from Amy.

The door banged and Mrs. March entered. "Merry Christmas, Marmee!" the girls cried together.

"Merry Christmas, daughters. I want to say one word before we sit down. Not far away from here is a woman named Mrs. Hummel and her baby and six children. They are suffering from hunger and cold. Will you give them your breakfast as a Christmas gift?"

They were all hungry, but they said yes and soon set out to bring the poor Hummel family a Christmas breakfast.

When they arrived, they built a fire with the wood they brought and spread the food on the table for the grateful children.

A Christmas Present from the Marches

When they returned home, they presented their mother with the gifts. Mrs. March was surprised and touched, and there was a good deal of laughing and hugging.

The rest of the day was devoted to preparations for the evening. When the girls went down to supper, they stared at the table in amazement. There was ice cream and cake and fruit and in the middle of the table, huge bouquets of fresh flowers.

Mrs. March said that Mr. Laurence, their neighbor, had sent all the goodies.

"The Laurence boy's grandfather! Why, we don't even know him," exclaimed Meg.

"Well," Mrs. March said, "he heard about your breakfast party and sent over a few trifles in honor of the day."

"The boy put it into his head. I know he did!" cried Jo. "He's such a good fellow, I wish we could get to know him."

Mr. Laurence and his grandson lived next

The Marches' Christmas Table

door, but the March girls hardly knew the boy. Everyone said the grandfather kept the boy inside with his tutor, Mr. Brooke, and made him study all the time.

"When the cat ran away, he brought her back," said Jo. "And I've talked with him over the fence. I want to get to know him. I think he needs some fun."

They talked about it while they ate the ice, and everyone agreed they had never seen such beautiful flowers.

Jo Thinks About the Laurence Boy.

"What Shall We Wear?"

Chapter 3
The Laurence Boy

"Jo, where are you?" cried Meg. "We have just received an invitation to a little holiday dance. Marmee said we may go, but what *shall* we wear?"

"We shall wear our cotton dresses, for they're the only ones we've got," answered Jo practically. "Yours is fine, but mine is burned in the back."

"You must sit still then and keep your back out of sight," said Meg. "And you must behave. I'll give you a signal if I see you doing anything wrong."

The next night the two younger sisters helped the older girls get ready for the party. There was much running up and down, laughing and talking. Finally they were ready. Meg's high heeled slippers were very tight and hurt her. Jo said the hairpins were sticking into her head.

When they arrived at the party, they joined a group of girls, but Jo didn't care much for girls or gossip, so she wandered off. No one came to talk to her, and she couldn't move around because her burned dress would show.

She finally slipped into a corner that was curtained off and was surprised to see that another bashful person was already there. It was "the Laurence boy."

"Dear me, I didn't know anybody was in here," stammered Jo.

But the boy laughed and said pleasantly, "Don't mind me. Stay if you like."

"You live near us, don't you, Mr. Laurence?"

The Laurence Boy

LITTLE WOMEN

said Jo, trying to be polite.

"Next door," the boy said. "But I'm not Mr. Laurence, I'm only Laurie. My first name is Theodore, but I like Laurie better."

They were soon talking and laughing. Laurie felt at ease with Jo, and Jo liked "the Laurence boy" better than ever. She looked at him carefully. He was fifteen years old, and he had curly black hair, big black eyes, and a handsome nose.

Soon Meg beckoned to her sister, and Jo reluctantly followed her into a side room. Meg was holding her foot. "I've sprained my ankle. That stupid high heel turned, and I can hardly stand. How am I ever going to get home?"

"I'll ask Laurie. He'll go for a carriage," said Jo.

"Mercy no!" said Meg. "Don't ask or tell anyone." Jo then went off to get Meg some supper and ended up spilling coffee on her

"I've Sprained My Ankle!"

dress.

She heard a friendly voice behind her say, "Can I help you?" It was Laurie. Jo explained that she was bringing supper to Meg, who had hurt herself. Laurie was very helpful. He offered his grandfather's carriage to take the girls home, saying it was no trouble. When it was time to go, he rode up in front, so the sisters could talk over their adventures.

The morning after the party, everyone was out of sorts. Meg complained and Jo grumbled as they left the house. But the sight of their mother waving and smiling in the window when they turned back made them feel more cheerful.

When Mr. March lost his property in trying to help an unfortunate friend, the two older girls offered to go to work to help the family. Meg found a place as a nursery governess. But she was more fond of luxury than the others and found the family's poverty especially hard to bear.

Meg and Jo Leave for Work.

Something about Jo struck old Aunt March, who was lame and needed a companion. Taking care of a peppery old lady did not suit Jo at all, but she could not refuse. The real attraction about going to Aunt March's was her large library of fine books. The moment Aunt March took her nap or was busy with company, Jo hurried to this quiet place.

Jo wanted to do something splendid with her life, but meanwhile, she loved to read and be boyish. Her quick temper, sharp tongue and restless spirit were always getting her into trouble.

Beth was too bashful to go to school. She had tried it, but she suffered so much that now she did her lessons at home. She was a homey little creature and helped Hannah. Beth would weep every once in a while because she couldn't take music lessons or have a fine piano, but no one ever saw her.

If anybody had asked Amy what the

Jo Loved Aunt March's Library.

greatest trial of her life was, she would have answered, "My nose." She pinched and pulled it, but it always remained rather flat. Amy had a talent for drawing, and her teachers complained that she covered her slate and books with pictures. She was a great favorite with everyone and was well on her way to being spoiled, even though she had to wear her cousin's hand-me-down dresses.

Amy confided in Meg, and Meg took special care of her. By some strange attraction of opposites, Jo and Beth were drawn to each other. The two older girls loved one another very much, but each took one of the younger girls into her keeping and watched over her in her own way.

The Greatest Trial of Amy's Life

Jo Sees Laurie at the Window.

Chapter 4
Being Neighborly

A garden with a low hedge separated the March's house from Mr. Laurence's house. The Laurence house was a stately stone mansion, with a big coach house and well-kept grounds. Yet it seemed a lonely house, and few people went in and out except the old gentleman and his grandson.

Jo longed to go inside and get to know "the Laurence boy," who looked as if he'd like to be known. One day she spied his wistful face at an upper window.

"There he is," thought Jo, "poor boy! All

alone! He needs someone to play with!" So when she went out, she tossed a snowball up to the window and called out, "How do you do? Wouldn't you like some nice girl to come over and amuse you?"

"I don't know any," he answered.

"You know us," said Jo and laughed.

"So I do. Will you come please?" cried Laurie.

Presently Jo appeared with a covered dish. "Mother sent her love and wanted me to bring you some custard. It isn't anything, but everyone felt kindly and wanted to show it."

They sat down in Laurie's parlor to talk. "I'll talk all day if I get going," said Jo. "Beth says I never know when to stop."

Laurie knew who each of the girls was, which surprised Jo. "I often hear you calling to one another," he explained, "and when I'm alone, I can't help looking over at your house. I haven't any mother, you know," he added

Jo Comes to Visit.

sadly.

"I just wish you'd come over. We'd have such jolly times," she said. "Wouldn't your grandpa let you? We're not strangers, we're neighbors."

They talked on and on, and then Laurie asked Jo to come see the house and his grandpa's books. He led her from room to room. "What riches!" sighed Jo when they reached the library. She stood before a fine portrait of the old gentleman and never heard the door open.

"What have you been doing to this boy of mine?" said the gruff voice of Mr. Laurence. Poor Jo couldn't blush any redder. Although his voice was gruff, the gentleman's eyes twinkled.

"Only trying to be neighborly, sir," she said. "Laurie seems a little lonely."

"So he is, but tea is about to be served, so come down and go on being neighborly."

"What Have You Been Doing to My Boy?"

LITTLE WOMEN

The old gentleman did not say much as he drank his tea, but he watched the young people chatting away like old friends. He liked Jo, for her odd blunt ways suited him. And before she left, Laurie took her to the drawing room and played the grand piano while Jo listened.

When Jo got home and related her afternoon's adventures, Mrs. March said "her friend" was very welcome at the March house.

All sorts of nice things started to happen. Everyone liked Laurie, and what good times they had! Meg walked in the Laurence's conservatory, Jo browsed in the library, and Amy copied pictures.

But Beth could not pluck up courage to go to the "mansion" and play the grand piano. She was afraid of gruff Mr. Laurence, but when he heard about this, he set to mending matters.

Laurie Plays the Grand Piano.

He sat in the March's parlor and led the conversation to music. "Wouldn't some of you girls like to run over and practice on the piano, just to keep it in tune? You needn't say anything to anybody, but run in at any time."

This was too much of a temptation for Beth. Next day, after two or three tries, she went in the side door and made her way noiselessly to the drawing room to play. She stayed until dinnertime and then could only sit and smile at everyone. After that, she slipped through the hedge nearly every day.

A few weeks later, she decided to make Mr. Laurence a pair of slippers to show her special thanks. She wrote a simple note and, with Laurie's help, got them smuggled into the old gentleman's study.

The next day passed, and the next, and Beth went out to do an errand. When she came back, her sisters led her to the parlor.

Beth Enters the Drawing Room.

There stood a little piano, with a letter addressed to Miss Elizabeth March.

"For me?" gasped Beth, holding onto Jo.

"Yes, all for you. Don't you think he's the dearest old man in the world? Try it. Let's hear the sound of the piano."

So Beth tried it, and everyone said it was the most remarkable piano they ever heard.

"You'll have to go and thank him," said Jo, though she didn't think Beth would ever go.

"Yes, I guess I'll go now, before I get frightened thinking about it." And to the family's amazement, Beth walked through the hedge and into the Laurence's door.

Beth knocked at the study door and with a trembling voice said, "I came to thank you, sir, for—" but she forgot her speech and put her arms round his neck. And from that moment she stopped fearing the gruff Mr. Laurence.

Beth Thanks Mr. Laurence.

Amy Wants to Go Too.

Chapter 5
Jo and Her Temper

"Girls, where are you going?" asked Amy, finding Jo and Meg getting ready to go out.

"Never mind. Little girls shouldn't ask questions," returned Jo.

"I know!" said Amy. "You're going to the theatre with Laurie! Oh, please, let me come too!"

"If she goes, I won't. Laurie only invited us," said Jo crossly. Amy wailed, which made Jo even more cross.

Just as they were setting out, Amy called down the stairs in a threatening tone, "You'll be sorry for this, Jo March! See if you're not!"

They had a splendid time, although several times Jo thought of her quick temper and how she tried to control it.

When they got home, they found Amy reading in the parlor. Jo took a quick look around her room, but everything seemed to be in place.

There Jo was mistaken, for the next day, she discovered that her writing book had disappeared.

"Amy, you've got it," she said.

"No, I haven't."

"You know where it is then," cried Jo, giving her a shake. "You'd better tell or I'll make you!"

"You'll never get it back," cried Amy, getting very excited. "I burned it up!"

"What! My book with all my writing in it?" said Jo, turning pale.

"Yes, I told you I'd make you pay—" Amy

Jo Gives Amy a Shake.

got no further for Jo shook her until her teeth chattered, crying:

"You wicked, wicked girl! I'll never forgive you as long as I live," and she rushed out of the room.

Jo's book was the pride of her heart, and she had worked over all the stories in it carefully. Amy's bonfire had burned up several years of work.

When the bell rang for tea, Jo appeared and Amy asked for forgiveness. "I shall never forgive you" was Jo's stern reply, and she said nothing more all evening.

Nothing went well the next day either, so Jo decided to ask Laurie to go skating. "He is always kind and jolly and will make me happier," she thought, and off she went.

Amy heard the sound of skates and, wanting to go very badly, decided to follow. It was not far to the river, but both Laurie and Jo had their skates on before Amy reached

Laurie and Jo Had Their Skates On.

them. Jo saw her and turned her back. Laurie went on ahead, testing the ice, for the weather had been warm. As he turned the bend, he shouted back, "Keep near the shore. It isn't safe in the middle."

Jo heard, but Amy was struggling to her feet and didn't hear a word.

Laurie was way ahead, Jo was just at the turn, and Amy was skating toward the middle. There was a strange feeling in Jo's heart, and something made her turn just in time to see Amy throw up her hands and crash through the soft ice. She tried to yell for Laurie; she tried to rush forward.

Laurie was by her in a flash, calling, "Bring a rail, quick!"

How she did it she didn't know. But while Laurie, lying flat, held Amy up by his arm, she got a rail from the fence and together they got her out.

Amy, shivering, dripping and crying, was

Amy Crashes Through the Ice.

bundled in Laurie's coat and rushed home. In no time, she was asleep before the warm fire.

Jo had hardly spoken. She looked pale and wild, and later dropped at her mother's side. "It's my dreadful temper," she cried. "If she had died, it would have been my fault."

"Well, you have learned a lesson," said her mother. "My temper used to be worse than yours, but I have learned to check it. I am angry nearly every day, but I do not show it. Your father has helped me."

It made them both sad to think of Father, and they held each other. Then Jo hugged Amy, who stirred in her sleep and hugged her back.

Jo Blames Her Dreadful Temper.

Helping Meg Pack Her Trunk

Chapter 6
Meg Tries to Be Fashionable

In April, Meg's friend, Annie Moffat, invited her for a two-week stay. The Moffats were very fashionable, and Mrs. March was afraid Meg's head would be turned.

The other girls helped her pack her trunk. There were going to be several small parties and a large party on Thursday. In went her old and mended white cotton party dress, along with her other everyday dresses and her old bonnet.

After Meg was at the Moffat's a few days, she began to imitate those around her and put on airs. The more she saw Annie Moffat's things, the more she envied her and sighed to be rich.

When the evening for one of the small parties came, out came Meg's old "ball dress," looking shabbier than ever. Meg saw the girls glance at it and then at one another, and her cheeks began to burn.

Then the maid came in with a box of flowers for Meg, and the girls gathered around, wanting to know who they were from.

"The note is from Mother, and the flowers are from Laurie," Meg said. Annie gave her sister a funny look. "He often sends us flowers; my mother and old Mr. Laurence are friends, you know." Meg felt almost happy again and enjoyed herself very much that evening. She didn't know why, but the next day the Moffat girls seemed to treat her with more interest and respect. They told her they'd sent an invitation to the young Mr. Laurence for Thursday's party.

Meg laughed, saying, "Laurie is only a little boy." Again the sisters exchanged looks.

Flowers for Meg

Annie's sister offered Meg her blue silk dress for Thursday's party, and on Thursday evening they made Meg into a fine lady. They laced her into the dress, which was very tight, crimped her hair, and gave her earrings and high heeled boots.

"I'm afraid to go down, I feel so stiff and half dressed," said Meg to Annie. But she acted the part of a fine lady though the tight dress gave her a side ache and she kept tripping over the train.

She was flirting and laughing when she saw Laurie staring at her with surprise. "I'm glad you came," she said to him in her most grown-up way.

"Jo wanted me to come and tell her how you looked," replied Laurie.

"Well, wouldn't Jo stare if she saw me? Do you like me dressed up like this?"

"No, I don't" was his blunt reply.

That was altogether too much from a lad

Meg Flirts at the Party.

younger than she. Meg walked away and stood by a window, where she overheard a gentleman saying, "They are making a fool of that little girl, dressing her like a doll."

"Oh dear," thought Meg, "I should have worn my own things."

"Laurie," she whispered when he asked her to dance, "please do me a favor and don't tell them at home about my dress. I'd rather tell them myself how silly I've been. I feel horrid. I only wanted a little fun, but I've found this doesn't pay."

Laurie agreed, but he was not pleased at the change he saw in her.

Meg was sick from too much champagne all the next day and found that she had not enjoyed herself as much as she expected. On Saturday she went home, and home seemed like a very nice place, even if it wasn't splendid.

Meg told her adventures to everyone. She

Meg Admits She Has Been Silly.

confessed later to Jo and her mother that she had allowed the Moffat girls to dress her up, and that she had romped and flirted after drinking too much champagne.

She also told them bits of gossip, especially one part she'd overheard about Mrs. March having "plans" for Laurie and her daughters because he was rich.

Jo said it was all rubbish, and Mrs. March ended by telling what her plans were:

"I want my daughters to be admired, loved and respected; to be well and to lead useful lives; and to marry only for love and happiness."

Meg Tells About the Gossip.

Beth, the Postmistress

Chapter 7
Summer and Dreams

Spring came, and gardening, walks, rowing on the river, and flower hunts filled the lengthening days.

To promote friendly relations between households, Laurie set up a post office made out of an old bird house in the hedge between the two houses.

The post office was very well used by everyone, even Mr. Laurence. Beth was postmistress. She was always home, and she liked the job of distributing the mail.

One day, Jo got an invitation from Laurie

to a picnic at Longmeadow with some of his English friends and Mr. Brooke, his tutor. The girls were invited for lunch and croquet.

Meg thought her dress of printed cotton would be just the thing. Beth said she would come if Jo promised not to let any of the boys talk to her. "I like to please Laurie," she added, "and I'm not afraid of Mr. Brooke. I'll work hard and not trouble anyone."

The sun shone brightly the next morning, and all the girls were making their own preparations. Amy had slept all night with a clothespin on her nose to try to give it a little uplift. Beth kept reporting what was going on next door. She saw the carriage full of people arrive and urged the girls to hurry.

"Oh, Jo, you're not going to wear that awful hat," said Meg as they were leaving.

"I just will," said Jo. "I don't mind being a boy, and this hat is fun." And with that, Jo marched off followed by the others.

Off for the Picnic at Longmeadow

Laurie ran to meet them and presented his friends. The party was soon ready to board the two boats.

Mr. Brooke and Ned Moffat rowed one boat, and Laurie and Jo rowed the other. The two friends were always together and shared a special friendship. Jo had a pet name for Laurie, which only she used. She called him Teddy.

Jo's funny hat produced a laugh from all, but Kate, the oldest of Laurie's English guests, looked amazed at everything Jo did.

Meg, in the other boat, faced Mr. Brooke, Laurie's tutor. He was a grave, silent young man, with handsome brown eyes and a pleasant voice. Meg liked his quiet manners and considered him to have a great store of useful knowledge. He never talked to her much, but he looked at her a great deal.

It was not far to Longmeadow. As they landed, Laurie suggested a game of croquet.

Meg Faces Mr. Brooke.

They then had lunch, and a very merry one it was. Cups and plates were overturned, acorns dropped into the milk, and little ants and caterpillars attended.

When lunch was over, Kate, Meg and Mr. Brooke—the older people—sat apart. Kate had a sketch pad and Mr. Brooke lay on the grass with a book.

Kate asked Meg if she went to school, and Meg replied, "No, I'm a governess."

"Oh, indeed," Kate said, but she might as well have said, "How dreadful!"

Mr. Brooke looked up and said quickly, "Young ladies in America are very independent. They are admired and respected for supporting themselves."

"Oh, yes, of course," said Kate, getting up. "How odd these Americans are," she thought. "I hope Laurie won't be spoiled among them."

"I forgot that English people turn up their noses at governesses and don't treat them as

Meg Is Annoyed.

we do," said Meg with an annoyed expression when Kate walked away.

"Tutors also have a hard time of it there," said Mr. Brooke, smiling. "But I shan't be a tutor for long. Laurie goes to college next year and when he goes, I will join the army."

"Laurie and his grandfather and all of us will be very sorry to see you go," said Meg, but she could not help noticing the way he looked at her.

One day, when the vacation was nearly over, Laurie said to the girls, "I have so many dreams, it would be hard to choose the one I'd want. But I'll tell my favorite one if you all will tell yours."

They agreed. So Laurie began:

"I'd like to see the world and then settle in Germany and be a famous musician."

Meg seemed to find it hard to tell hers, but she said, "I want a lovely house full of luxurious things and heaps of money."

Sharing Favorite Dreams

"You know your castle wouldn't be perfect without a good husband and some children," said Jo.

"You'd have nothing but inkstands and novels in yours," said Meg.

"Wouldn't I, though!" said Jo. "I want to do something special. I think I shall write books and get famous. That would suit me."

"My favorite dream is to stay home and take care of the family," said Beth. "Since I have my piano, I am satisfied."

"I want to be an artist and go to Rome and do fine pictures," said Amy.

Laurie was going to college in a few weeks. It was to please his grandfather, but he said he sometimes felt like breaking away and pleasing himself.

Jo, who was always ready with a plan, said, "If we are all alive in ten years, let's meet and see how many of us have got our wishes." And they all agreed.

Planning a Meeting in Ten Years

Jo Takes Her Manuscripts to the City.

Chapter 8
Secrets

When the fall came, Jo was busy in the garret, her special hideaway where she did all her writing. When she finished her manuscript, she took it and another one from the drawer, and crept down and out the door.

She went at a fast pace to the city and stood by a certain door, then gave herself a shake and went in. In ten minutes she came out looking as if she'd had a trying ordeal. Laurie was waiting for her. He had seen her leave in a determined manner and decided to follow.

"Why are you here alone? Are you up to some mischief, Jo?" said Laurie. "I have a secret to tell, but if I do, you must tell me why you're here."

"Well, Teddy, if you won't say anything at home or tease me, I'll tell," said Jo. "I've left two stories with a newspaperman, and he's going to tell me if he likes them next week."

"Hurrah for Miss March, the celebrated author!" shouted Laurie.

"Hush, it may not come to anything. But I had to try. Now tell me your secret."

"Brooke has Meg's glove," whispered Laurie. "Isn't it romantic?"

Jo looked displeased. "I wish you hadn't told me. I don't like the idea of anyone coming to take Meg away." Lately Jo had felt that Meg was getting to be a woman, and she dreaded the separation she knew was soon to come.

For the next two weeks, Jo behaved very strangely. She rushed to the door when the postman rang, was rude to Mr. Brooke, and whispered a lot to Laurie. Two Saturdays

Telling Secrets

later, Meg heard shrieks of laughter and a great flapping of newspapers from Jo and Laurie in the yard.

"What shall we do with that girl? She never will behave like a young lady," said Meg. In a few minutes Jo bounced in and offered to read a story from the paper. Everyone listened with interest, and then Jo couldn't resist announcing she had written it!

"You?" cried Meg.

"I knew it! I knew it! Oh, Jo, I'm so proud." Beth ran to hug her sister.

Then Jo told them to stop jabbering so she could tell the whole story. When her breath gave out, she wrapped her head in the paper and cried a few tears on it.

Jo's Story in the Newspaper!

Bad News

Chapter 9
A Telegram

November came, and the girls said it was the most disagreeable month in the year.

Meg sat at the table when Mrs. March came in with her usual, "Any letter from Father, girls? It's our day for a letter."

There was a sharp ring at the door, and Hannah came in with a telegram. Mrs. March snatched it, read it, and dropped back into her chair. Jo read aloud in a frightened voice:

"MRS. MARCH:

YOUR HUSBAND IS VERY ILL. COME AT ONCE TO WASHINGTON."

How still the room was. The whole world suddenly seemed to change. Mrs. March was herself again in a minute and said, "I shall go at once, but it may be too late."

First there was the sound of sobbing, but then everyone set about to help Mrs. March get ready. Laurie was to go send a telegram and drop off a note at Aunt March's. The money for the sad trip would have to be borrowed. It was decided that Mr. Brooke would go too. Everything was arranged by the time Laurie returned. But where was Jo? They began to worry when she burst in and laid a roll of bills before her mother.

"That's for making Father comfortable and bringing him home. I earned it. I only sold what was my own."

As she spoke, she took off her bonnet, and everyone saw that all her beautiful hair—the hair she was so proud of—was cut off and sold. They all exclaimed and Beth went to hug her.

Jo's Beautiful Hair Is Gone!

"What made you do it?" asked Amy, who would as soon have cut off her head as her pretty hair.

"I wanted to do something for Father. As I was passing a barber's window, I saw some hair pieces in there, and I knew I had one thing to make money out of. So I walked in and asked if he bought hair.

"The barber was not used to having girls bounce in his shop offering to sell their hair, but I begged him to take it."

Mrs. March thanked her, and they tried to talk of other things. No one wanted to go to bed that night. Beth went to the piano and played Father's favorite hymn.

Meg lay awake for hours when all of a sudden she heard a stifled sob. "My hair," Jo cried into her pillow. "It's vain and selfish, but I can't help it. It was my one beauty."

They had breakfast in the cold gray dawn. The trunk was ready in the hall. Nobody

The Barber Cut Jo's Hair.

talked much, but as they sat waiting for the carriage, Mrs. March said:

"Girls, I leave you to Hannah's care and Mr. Laurence's protection. Go on with your work as usual. Hope and keep busy. Meg, watch over your sisters. Be patient, Jo, and don't do rash things. Beth, comfort yourself with your music, and Amy, help all you can."

There was one hard minute. They kissed their mother and tried to wave cheerfully when she drove away.

News from their father comforted the girls. He was dangerously ill, but Mrs. March had already done him good. Mr. Brooke sent a bulletin every day, and they became more cheerful as the weeks passed.

Everyone was eager to write, and plump letters full of news and cheer were sent to Washington by the sisters.

A Hard Good-Bye

Beth Slips Out Alone.

Chapter 10
Dark Days

For a week after their mother left, the girls
ere as helpful as they could be. Beth kept
n, doing her own duties and many of her
isters' too.

Ten days after Mrs. March's departure,
eth tried to get one of her sisters to go with
er to visit poor families, as their mother had
one. "The Hummel baby is sick," she said,
and I don't know what to do for it."

Jo was reading a story, Meg went upstairs,
nd Amy did not come, so Beth silently
ipped out into the chilly air.

When Jo went upstairs later, she found

Beth looking very grave and ill.

"What's the matter?" cried Jo.

"Oh, Jo, Mrs. Hummel's baby died on m
lap while I was holding it. Scarlet fever!"

"How dreadful! I ought to have gone," sai
Jo taking her sister in her arms. "Oh, Betl
if you should be sick, I never could forgiv
myself."

"Don't be frightened," said Beth, whos
cheeks were flushed and forehead hot. '
shan't have it badly. I did take som
medicine, and I feel better."

"I'll call Hannah," said Jo. "She'll kno
what to do."

Hannah came and assured Jo there was n
need to worry. Everyone had scarlet fever.
treated right, no one died.

"We'll call Dr. Bangs and send Amy off 1
Aunt March's so she won't catch it. You an
Meg can stay at home."

When Amy was told, she cried and the

Scarlet Fever!

declared she'd rather have the fever than go to Aunt March. She became agreeable only when Laurie promised to come and take her for a ride every day.

Dr. Bangs said that Beth did have symptoms of fever. They decided not to tell Mrs. March, as she couldn't leave Father, and it would only make her worry.

Beth was much sicker than anyone but Hannah and the doctor suspected. She would wake and then sink back into the fever fits. She did not even recognize the familiar faces around her.

Still Mrs. March was not told. Jo devoted herself to Beth night and day. Laurie haunted the house like a ghost.

The first of December was a wintry day. When Dr. Bangs came that morning, he looked at Beth and said, "If Mrs. March can leave her husband, she'd better be sent for."

Jo snatched up a telegram and rushed out.

"Mrs. March Must Be Sent For."

"I've sent for Mother," she said to Laurie when she returned. "The doctor told us to."

"Oh, Jo, it's not so bad as that?" cried Laurie.

The tears started to stream down Jo's cheeks. Laurie held out his hand and whispered, "I'm here. Hold on to me, Jo dear. Keep hoping for the best. Your mother will be here soon, and everything will be all right. I telegraphed her yesterday, and she'll be here tonight." Soon Jo dried her eyes. Laurie beamed. "Aren't you glad I did it?"

Jo threw her arms around his neck, and Laurie patted her back. He even followed it up with a bashful kiss or two.

"I got Grandpa to say it was time we did something. The late train comes in at 2:00 A.M. I shall go for her."

A breath of fresh air seemed to blow through the house. Everyone rejoiced but Beth. All day long Meg and Jo hovered over

Laurie Comforts Jo.

her. The hours dragged by. The doctor came
and said some change would take place about
midnight.

The girls did not sleep that night. The
clock struck twelve. An hour went by. Nothing happened except Laurie's departure for
the station.

At two o'clock it looked to Jo as if a change
had taken place, so she woke Hannah, who
ran to Beth and exclaimed, "The fever has
broken. She's sleeping naturally. Praise be
given!"

Both girls crept into the dark hall and held
each other close. "If Mother would only
come," said Jo, as the sky started to lighten.

Then there was the sound of bells at the
door below and Laurie's voice crying, "Girls
she's come! Marmee's come!"

The Fever Has Broken!

A Hard Time at Aunt March's

Chapter 11
Serious Conversations

While these things were happening at home, Amy was having a hard time at Aunt March's. Aunt March took Amy in hand to teach her the way she had been taught sixty years ago.

Amy had to do all of Aunt's tiresome labors and read aloud after dinner. If it had not been for Laurie and old Esther, the maid, she felt she could not have gotten through. Esther took a fancy to Amy and let her examine all the curious and pretty things stored away in the big house. Amy's chief delight was a big cabinet full of jewelry. "I wish I knew where all these pretty things will go when Aunt March dies," Amy said to Esther, replacing the jewels.

"To you and your sisters. I have seen Madame's will," whispered Esther.

"How nice! But I wish she'd let us have them now," said Amy.

"It is too soon. But that little turquoise ring will be given to you when you go home, for Madame approves of you."

"Do you think so? I'll be very good if only I can have that ring. I do like Aunt March, after all," added Amy.

From that day on, she was a model of obedience, and the old lady thought her training was very successful.

But when Laurie came and said that Beth was in danger, Amy went and prayed for her, feeling that a million turquoise rings would not make up for losing her gentle sister.

Amy Wants the Turquoise Ring.

With Mother home, the house was full of genuine happiness. Beth woke from her sleep, and her eyes fell on her mother. Then she slept again, and Meg and Jo waited on their mother. They heard all the news of Father and Mr. Brooke, and then they closed their weary eyes to sleep. Mrs. March wouldn't leave Beth's side and rested in the big chair.

Laurie went off to keep Amy posted. But he fell asleep on the sofa after his long night and was awakened by Amy's cry of joy at the sight of her mother.

As Amy was talking, Mrs. March saw the ring on her hand. Amy said, "Aunt March gave me the ring today, and I'd like to wear it to remind me not to be selfish. Beth isn't selfish and that's why everyone loves her."

"Wear your ring, dear, and do your best," said Mrs. March. "Now I must get back to Beth."

That evening, Jo found her mother in

Amy Runs to Her Mother.

Beth's room and said, "I want to talk to you, Mother."

"About Meg?" questioned Mrs. March.

"Yes. How did you know? Mr. Brooke has one of Meg's gloves, and Teddy saw it and teased him. He said he liked Meg but didn't dare say anything because she was so young and he was so poor. I don't know anything about love and such nonsense!" cried Jo.

"Dear, don't get angry. John—that's what we call Mr. Brooke now—went with me and was very devoted to Father. He was very open about his love for Meg. He told us he wanted to marry her. He is an excellent young man, but I will not consent to Meg's marrying so young."

"Of course not! It would be idiotic. It's worse than I imagined!" cried Jo.

"Don't say anything to Meg," said Mrs. March. "I don't know whether she loves John yet. But I'll be able to judge better when I see

Jo Tells Marmee about Mr. Brooke.

them together."

"I see it all! When he comes back, it will all be settled. He will marry her and take her off and make a hole in our family," moaned Jo.

"Meg is only seventeen," said Mrs. March. "Your father and I have agreed that Meg shall not marry before she is twenty. If she and John love each other, they can wait."

Just then Meg entered the room with a letter she was writing to Father, and Mrs. March said, "Please add that I send my love to John."

"Do you call him 'John'?" asked Meg, smiling.

"Yes, he has been like a son to us," replied Mrs. March, looking at her daughter.

Meg only smiled and said, "Good night, Mother dear. It is so comfortable to have you home."

A Letter for Father

A Christmas Snow Maiden for Beth

Chapter 12
Aunt March Settles the Question

As Christmas neared, both invalids improved. Mr. March wrote that he would soon be home with them, and Beth was brought downstairs to lie on the sofa all day.

On Christmas morning, Beth was carried to the window to see the stately snow maiden Jo and Laurie had made during the night. Laurie ran up and down bringing in the gifts.

"I'm so full of happiness that if Father were here, I couldn't hold one drop more," said Beth.

Half an hour later, Laurie opened the parlor door and in a breathless voice said,

"Here's another present for the Marches."

There in the doorway was a tall man, leaning on the arm of another tall man. For several minutes everybody seemed to lose their wits. Then they ran to embrace Mr. March. Jo nearly fainted and had to be tended to by Laurie. Mr. Brooke kissed Meg entirely by mistake. Amy sobbed on her father's boots.

Then the study door flew open, and Beth ran straight into her father's arms.

Mr. March told them how he had wanted to surprise them, and when the fine weather came, he and Mr. Brooke took advantage of it to return home.

There was a gay Christmas dinner that night with the family, Mr. Laurence and his grandson, and Mr. Brooke. After dinner, the family sat around the fire.

"Just a year ago we were groaning, remember?" asked Jo.

"It's been a rather rough road for you to

Another Present for the Marches

travel," said Mr. March, looking at the four faces, "but you have got on bravely." Mr. March then praised each of them—Meg for her hard work, Jo for how ladylike and gentle she had become, Beth for not being as shy as she used to be, and Amy for thinking of other people more and herself less.

Then, for the first time in many months, Beth went slowly to her place at the little piano for the evening song.

The next day, there was a strange feeling in the house. Meg was absent-minded, shy and silent, and blushed when John's name was mentioned.

She told Jo that she would act very calm if Mr. Brooke did propose. But a tap on the door made her lose her dignity entirely, and she started sewing furiously.

It *was* Mr. Brooke, and Jo slipped out of the room. Meg rose to go and started to murmur, but Mr. Brooke took her hand.

Meg Tries to Act Calm.

"Oh, please don't go, Meg. I won't trouble you, I only want to know if you care for me a little. I love you so."

This was the moment for the calm proper speech, but Meg just hung her head and answered, "I don't know." John begged and Meg faltered. He was grave and pale, but tender.

It was at this moment that Aunt March hobbled into the room. She had heard Mr. March was home and had rushed over.

"Bless me, what's this?" cried the old lady as Mr. Brooke left the room.

"It's Father's friend," stammered Meg. "I'm so surprised to see you."

"There's mischief going on and I want to know what it is. Tell me, do you mean to marry this man? If you do, not one penny of my money ever goes to you!"

"I'll marry whom I please, Aunt March," said Meg, raising her chin.

"Highty-tighty! Is that the way you take

Aunt March Enters.

my advice? It's your duty to marry well and help your family. But I see you intend to marry a man without money, position or business. I thought you had more sense."

"We are willing to work, and we mean to wait. I'm not afraid of being poor. I know I shall be happy because he loves me."

Aunt March was very angry. She had counted on making a good match for pretty Meg. "Well, I wash my hands of the whole affair. I'm disappointed in you and haven't the heart to see your father now. Don't expect anything from me when you're married."

She slammed the door in Meg's face and drove off. Mr. Brooke came running in.

"I couldn't help hearing, Meg. It proves that you do care for me a little bit."

Fifteen minutes after Aunt March's departure, Jo came softly downstairs and stopped dead at the scene she saw. Meg was sitting on John's knee, looking blissful. Jo gasped,

Aunt March Is Very Angry.

and John said, "Sister Jo, congratulate us!"

This was too much! Jo ran upstairs and told her mother and father what she'd seen. Then she told the awful news to Beth and Amy, who both considered it a most agreeable event. Later Laurie came prancing in, bearing a big bouquet for "Mrs. John Brooke."

"You don't look festive," he said to Jo. "What's the matter?"

"You don't know how hard it is for me to give up Meg," she said with a quiver in her voice.

"You don't have to give her up, even though it will never be the same. You've got me, and I'll stand by you, Jo."

"I know you will, Teddy," returned Jo, "and it will be three years till she's twenty," she added thoughtfully.

"Don't you wish you could look forward and see where we all will be then? I do."

A Bouquet for "Mrs. John Brooke"

Mr. March Comes Home to His Books.

Chapter 13
The First Wedding

The three years that passed brought few changes to the family. The war ended, and Mr. March came home to his books.

John Brooke joined the army for a year and then prepared for business and earning a home for Meg.

Meg spent her time working and waiting, and only occasionally felt disappointed at how humble her life was beginning.

Jo never went back to Aunt March. The old lady took a fancy to Amy and offered her drawing lessons as a bribe. Jo devoted herself to writing and to Beth, who remained delicate long after the fever was over. Jo still wrote romances for the newspaper, but she had great plans in her brain.

Laurie went to college to please his grandfather, but did not work hard. He brought home the fellows from his class, and Amy became quite the favorite among them. They all liked Jo, but never fell in love with her.

Mr. Brooke found a tiny, charming house for Meg's first home. It had simple furniture, plenty of books, flowers on the windowsill, and pretty gifts made by the sisters. Jo and her mother put away Meg's few boxes, barrels and bundles. Hannah helped set up the kitchen, and Laurie brought a new gadget every week. The contents of the well-stocked linen closet were from Aunt March, who had not really meant what she said.

On the day before the wedding, Laurie appeared for his weekly visit and reported that

Setting Up Meg's First Home

John had gone for the license and Hannah was just taking in the cake.

Jo and he walked home arm in arm. "Now Teddy," she said, "I want to talk seriously to you about tomorrow. You must promise to behave well. No pranks."

Laurie promised, and Jo sighed, "Well, at least we won't have any more weddings for a while. I think it's dreadful breaking up families."

"Mark my words, you'll go next, Jo," said Laurie.

"No, I'm not the agreeable sort. Nobody will want me."

"You won't give anybody a chance," said Laurie, a little color rising in his cheeks. "When anybody does see the soft side of you, you throw cold water on him."

"I don't like that sort of thing. I'm too busy to be worried with nonsense, so let's change the subject," said Jo crossly.

"You'll be Married Next, Jo."

The wedding day dawned cloudless and rosy. Meg looked like a rose herself. She had made her wedding gown, and the only ornaments she wore were lilies of the valley, John's favorite flower. She rushed about with last minute preparations, but found time to hug each sister.

There was to be no ceremonious performance. Everything was to be as natural and homelike as possible. When Aunt March arrived, she was shocked to see the bride come running to welcome her. Jo upset the cake just as the house was filling with guests.

A silence fell on the room as the couple took their place under the green arch. Mother and sisters gathered close, but Meg looked straight up into her husband's eyes and said, "I will."

Jo did not cry, though she came very close, and only stopped when she felt Laurie's eyes upon her.

Meg Says, "I Will."

The minute after she was married, Meg cried, "The first kiss for Marmee!" and ran to her mother.

There was a lunch of cake and fruit, and then people strolled around through the house and garden. When she was ready to leave, Aunt March said to Meg, "I wish you well, my dear, but I think you'll be sorry for it," and added to the bridegroom, "You've got a treasure, young man, see that you deserve it."

The little house was not far away, and the only bridal journey Meg had was a walk with John from the old house to the new. They all gathered around her to say good-bye.

"I expect to keep my old place in all your hearts even though I am married. You'll all drop in and be with me a great deal. Thank you all for my happy wedding day."

From the Old House to the New

Amy's Artistic Endeavors

Chapter 14
Endeavors

Amy attempted every branch of art with enthusiasm. She devoted herself first to pen and ink drawing, then oil painting, and then charcoal portraits. After this, she went to plaster casts until one day she tried to cast her own foot, and they found her hopping around with her foot in a pan full of hardened plaster. With much difficulty, she was dug out, but Jo was so overcome with laughter, she cut Amy's foot by accident.

Amy was learning, doing and enjoying other things meanwhile, for she had resolved to be an attractive and accomplished woman. She made friends easily and took life gracefully. She had a sense of what was pleasing and proper and knew the right thing to say to each person.

One of her weaknesses, however, was a desire to move in the best society. She considered money, position and elegant manners most desirable, and she and Jo often argued about such questions.

"You don't care to make people like you, or to go into good society. I do, and I mean to make the most of every chance that comes. You can go about with your nose in the air and your elbows out if you like."

Jo did not think herself a genius by any means, but when the "writing fit" came on, she would shut herself in her room and write with her heart and soul. During these periods, the family kept their distance. The writing fits didn't last long, and then she

In a "Writing Fit"

emerged, hungry, sleepy and cross.

Jo attended a lecture one evening and sat next to a lad reading a newspaper. Jo started looking at it, and when he turned the page, the boy offered her half of his paper, saying, "Want to read it? It's a first-rate story."

The story was full of love, mystery, murder and disaster. "I think you or I could do as well if we tried," said Jo, amused that he liked the story so well.

"I would feel pretty lucky if I could! The author of these makes a good living from stories. She knows what folks like and gets paid well for writing it."

Jo took down the address of the paper and resolved to try for the hundred-dollar prize offered for the most sensational story.

She said nothing of her plan, but went to work the next day. She sent off the story and waited for six weeks. When she was just giving up hope, a letter arrived with a check for

Jo Resolves to Try for the Prize.

one hundred dollars. There was a grand jubilee when she told the family.

"What will you do with such a fortune?" asked Amy.

"Send Beth and Mother to the seaside for a month or two!" answered Jo promptly.

To the seaside they went. Beth didn't come back as plump and rosy as could be desired, but she was better. Jo earned several more checks, and the magic of her pen paid the bills and bought a new carpet.

Then Jo decided to submit her novel for publication. In hopes of pleasing everyone, she took all of their advice and ended up suiting nobody. The novel was printed, and she got three hundred dollars for it, but she wasn't satisfied and decided not to write another till she felt ready.

A Grand Jubilee!

Meg's Jelly Won't Jell.

Chapter 15
Domestic Experiences

Right away Meg was determined to be a model housekeeper. One thing she wanted to do was fill her storeroom with homemade preserves. The currants on their bush were ripe, and John sent home jars and sugar. She had seen Hannah make jelly a dozen times, and she spent a long day picking, boiling, and fussing over her jelly. But it wouldn't jell. At five o'clock, Meg sat down in the topsy-turvy kitchen and wept.

It was on this day that John decided to bring a friend home to dinner unannounced.

When they arrived home, there was not a soul around the house. John hurried in, led by the smell of burned sugar.

Meg sobbed dismally in the kitchen. "Oh, John, I'm so tired and hot and cross! I've been at it till I'm worn out."

"Has something dreadful happened?" asked the anxious John.

"The jelly won't jell, and I don't know what to do!" wailed Meg. John laughed and told Meg that he had brought a friend to dinner.

"Take him away at once!" cried Meg. "I can't see him and there isn't any dinner! I meant to go to Mother's!"

"Don't cry," soothed John. "If you lend a hand, everything will be all right. Give us cold meat and bread and cheese; we won't ask for jelly!"

He meant it as a joke, but Meg thought it was cruel. She dropped her apron and went to cry in her room.

A Cruel Joke

When Meg came down, the men had eaten and strolled away together. John came back after seeing his friend off, and they each sat, expecting the other to apologize first.

"Oh, dear," thought Meg, "married life is very trying." But she then decided she would say "forgive me" and went slowly across the room. She kissed her husband on the forehead. Then John said solemnly:

"It was bad of me to laugh at the jelly. I never will again."

In the autumn, Meg and her old friend Sallie, who had married a rich man, spent a lot of time together. Seeing Sallie's pretty things made Meg long for them and pity herself.

Meg knew where John's money was and could take as much as she liked as long as she could account for it once a month in her little account books.

Two days before settling up day, Sallie had been buying silks, and Meg, counting on

Meg Longs for Pretty Things.

twenty-five dollars from Aunt March for New Year's, took twenty-five dollars from the household fund and bought some too. It was a foolish thing to do, and it haunted her.

When John got out his books that night, Meg's heart sank. "Dear John, I'm afraid to show you my book for I've been very extravagant lately. In addition to trifles, I've spent fifty dollars for a silk dress."

For a moment the room was very still.

"I know you are angry, John, but I can't help it. I can't resist when I see Sallie buying all she wants. I try to be contented, but I'm tired of being poor."

The last words were spoken so low she thought he did not hear them. But he did, and they hurt him.

"I was afraid of this, Meg," he said, standing up. "I do my best."

She ran to him and held him close and said she didn't mean it. He forgave her, and the

Settling-Up Day at the Brooke's

next day Meg went to Sallie and told her the truth and asked her to buy the silk as a favor. Sallie did, and then gave it to Meg a while later as a present.

The year rolled around, and then mid-summer, and then Meg had twins—a boy and a girl. "Twins, by Jupiter!" was all Laurie could say when he came rushing over. "Isn't it fun? I was never more staggered in my life!"

The boy was named John Laurence, and the girl Margaret, after her mother and grandmother.

"We shall call her Daisy, so as not to have two Megs," said Amy.

"Name him Demijohn, and call him 'Demi' for short!" shouted Laurie.

"Daisy and Demi—just the thing! I knew Teddy would do it," said Jo, clapping her hands. And the babies were known as Daisy and Demi from then on.

Daisy and Demi

Amy Gives Instructions.

Chapter 16
Calls

"Come, Jo, you promised to make calls with me today," said Amy. Jo hated calls of the formal sort and never went until Amy made her.

Jo sighed, but got up to get dressed.

"I'm perfectly miserable, but if you consider me presentable, that's enough."

Amy gave the instructions as they walked:

"The Chesters consider themselves very elegant, so be on your best behavior. Just be calm, cool and quiet—you can do it for fifteen minutes."

Jo took her at her word and sat silent.

Amy tried in vain to make her talk.

"What a haughty, uninteresting girl the elder Miss March is," they heard someone say as they left.

Amy's next instructions to Jo were to be sociable, but she felt anxious, for when Jo turned freakish, there was no knowing when she'd stop.

At the next house, Jo told stories which embarrassed Amy, and in dismay, Amy told her she was washing her hands of Jo.

So Jo enjoyed herself on the next call. There were boys there, and Jo listened to their college stories, sat on the grass, and played with the children.

Their last call was at Aunt March's. Jo wanted to go home, but Amy insisted that they go because Aunt liked it.

Jo said she would show her disapproval of things and people whenever she felt like it, but Amy calmed her down, telling her not to

Jo Enjoys Herself.

worry Aunt with her new ideas.

"I'll try not to," replied Jo, "but I always feel like bursting out with a blunt speech or shocking remark. It's my doom."

They found another aunt, Aunt Carrol, with the old lady. Jo was not in a good mood, but Amy pleased everybody.

During the conversation, Jo said, "I don't like favors, they make me feel like a slave. I'd rather be independent."

"Ahem," coughed Aunt Carrol with a look at Aunt March. Jo sat with her nose in the air.

"Do you speak French, dear?" Aunt Carrol asked Amy later. Amy nodded, but Jo said she couldn't bear French. She thought it a silly language.

Another look passed between the two aunts. Jo brought the visit to an end and shook hands, but Amy kissed both aunts.

A week later, a letter came from Aunt

The Aunts Exchange Looks.

Carrol. She was going abroad soon.

"And she wants me to go with her!" burst in Jo, flying out of her chair.

"No, dear, not you, it's Amy," said Mother.

"Oh, Mother, she's too young! It's my turn first—I *must* go!"

"I'm afraid it's impossible. Aunt says Amy. She says that 'favors burden you' and that you 'hate French.' "

"Oh, my tongue! Why can't I learn to keep it quiet?" moaned Jo.

"Jo dear, I'm very selfish, but I couldn't spare you, and I'm glad you're not going," whispered Beth.

Jo bore up well until Amy left, and she then fled to her attic and cried till she couldn't cry any more.

Amy clung to Laurie at the last minute and he told her, "I'll come and comfort you if anything happens," little dreaming that he would.

Last Minute Fears

A Change in Beth

Chapter 17
Jo's Friend

"Jo, I'm anxious about Beth," said Mrs. March. "It's not her health; it's her spirits. She sits alone and cries a good deal. Now and then I see a look in her face I don't understand."

Jo said thoughtfully, "I think she's growing up. Why, Mother, Beth's eighteen, but we don't realize it. We treat her like a child."

"So we do. I leave Beth to your hands. I depend on you so, Jo," Mrs. March answered.

Jo watched Beth and finally settled on an idea which seemed to explain the change.

LITTLE WOMEN

One day Beth was watching Laurie go by outside, and Jo saw a tear drop from her eye.

"Mercy on me, Beth loves Laurie!" thought Jo. "Oh, dear, we are growing up. Here's Meg married and a mamma, Amy in Europe, and Beth in love!" She sighed, because everyone in the family felt that Laurie was getting fonder than ever of her. Jo, of course, wouldn't hear of the subject.

Jo watched Laurie that night. Nothing unusual happened—Beth was quiet and Laurie was very kind to her. But Jo thought she saw all kinds of things. Laurie soon sat down next to her.

"Come, Jo, be nice," said Laurie. "After studying all week, I need to be cared for."

"Go to Beth, I'm busy" was her answer.

"No, she's not to be bothered with me. I'd do anything for you, Jo, if you'd let me."

"Now you're flirting," said Jo. "Although you don't see any harm in it, I just can't

"Beth In Love?"

learn how it's done. I've tried, but I don't seem to get on. Not like Amy."

"I'm glad you can't flirt. It's good to see a sensible, straightforward girl who can be both jolly and kind."

"If you must, Teddy," said Jo, dropping her voice, "go and devote yourself to one of the pretty modest girls you do respect."

"I'd rather stay here with you," he said, winding Jo's apron tassel around his finger.

"I thought you hated to be tied to a woman's apron string," Jo retorted.

"That depends on who wears the apron," said Laurie as he fled.

Jo lay awake long that night and was just dropping to sleep when she heard stifled sobs. She flew to Beth's side. "What is it, dear? Is it the old pain?"

"No, it's a new one. But you can't cure it. There is no cure." Beth clung to her sister and cried and then laid her head in Jo's lap.

Tied to Jo's Apron Strings!

Jo was frightened. Even though she thought she knew the cause of Beth's pain, she said:

"Wouldn't it be a comfort to tell me what it is?"

"Not now, not yet."

"Then I won't ask. But remember that Mother and I are always glad to hear and help you."

"I'll tell you by and by," whispered Beth. And so they both went to sleep.

But Jo had made up her mind, and a few days later she told her mother that she wanted to go away for the winter. She needed a change and felt anxious and restless. Jo's idea was to go to New York. Her mother's friend, Mrs. Kirke, had written asking for a young person to teach her children and to sew.

Jo said to her mother slowly, "It may be vain and wrong of me to say it, but—I'm afraid Laurie is getting too fond of me."

"Then you don't care for him in the way he

Jo Comforts Beth.

cares for you?"

"Mercy no! I love the dear boy as I always have, but as for anything more than that, no. I think I had better go away before it comes to anything. Beth can comfort him when I'm gone and cure him of this romantic notion."

Mrs. Kirke gladly accepted Jo. Trembling with fear, she told Laurie about her plans. He took it very quietly and Jo was relieved. But when he said good-bye, he whispered, "It won't do a bit of good, Jo. My eye is on you, so mind what you do."

Mrs. Kirke had a big house and gave Jo the sky parlor, where she could sit and write. The two little girls she was to teach were pretty children.

Soon after Jo arrived, she heard a gentleman with a foreign accent. Later Mrs. Kirke told her that this boarder was Mr. Friedrich Bhaer, from Berlin. He was rather stout, with hair tumbling over his head, a bushy

Mr. Bhaer

beard, kind eyes, and a splendid big voice. He looked like a gentleman though his coat had buttons missing and his shoe was patched.

All the children in the house loved him, and he helped them with their German and often frolicked with them.

Jo spent her days teaching, sewing and writing in her cozy room. She picked up some more bits of news about Mr. Bhaer and was introduced to him by the little girls.

She met him on her way out one day, standing in the doorway of his room holding a sock and a darning needle.

She laughed all the way downstairs, but thought it was sad that he had to mend his own clothes.

Jo met Mr. Bhaer's nephews, Emil and Franz, and thought they were jolly little lads, quite after her own heart.

Mrs. Kirke called Jo one day as she passed Mr. Bhaer's room. "Did you ever see such a

Mr. Bhaer Mends His Own Clothes.

den, my dear? Come and help me. I've been trying to find out what he has done to his handkerchiefs!" Jo went into the topsy-turvy room. Books and papers were everywhere.

"Such a man!" laughed Mrs. Kirke. "I agreed to do his washing and mending, but he forgets to put his things out."

"Let me mend them," said Jo. "He seems to be such a kind man."

So Jo got his things in order and mended all his socks. Nothing was said, but one day Mr. Bhaer came up to her.

"Have you a wish to learn German?"

"Yes," she said, "but you are too busy."

"I have a debt to pay, Miss March." He pointed to the sewing. "You think I'm stupid that I don't see what you do? I have eyes and I see much. Come, a little lesson now and then in return." So they made the bargain.

On New Year's Day, Mr. Bhaer gave Jo a book because he knew she loved books. Not

Straightening Up the Topsy-Turvy Room

having much money, Jo got him several little useful things and put them around his room.

Though very busy, Jo still found time for her writing. Her fondest wish was to fill the house with comforts, give Beth everything she wanted, and go abroad herself. She again took to writing "sensation stories" because they paid well.

She took a story to the *Weekly Volcano,* a paper which printed those kind of stories. The editor agreed to publish it, and he told Jo if she wanted to write more, to make them short and spicy. Her stories filled the columns of the *Weekly Volcano,* but her name never appeared, and she told no one. She was saving the money she got for them to take Beth to the mountains next summer.

Eager to find material for her stories, Jo studied all manner of people, among them, Mr. Bhaer. Everyone liked him, though he was neither great nor handsome. Jo often

Finding a Publisher for Her Stories

watched him, trying to discover his charm. He was always kind, pleasant and cheery. Though poor, he always seemed to be giving something away. He never spoke of himself, and no one ever knew that in his native city he had been a highly respected professor.

Her belief in him strengthened daily. She wanted his respect and friendship. One day when they were having a conversation, it came out that Mr. Bhaer found the papers which printed sensation stories disgusting.

Jo blushed at this, and Mr. Bhaer noticed it. He knew that Jo wrote, but he asked her no questions about her work. He had seen her downtown where the newspaper offices were. And now it suddenly occurred to him that she was doing work she could not be proud of. Jo also felt that she should not be wasting her time writing this trash just because there was a market for it.

When she went to her room, she got out

Mr. Bhaer Doesn't Like Sensation Stories.

her papers and stuffed them into her stove. After that, she wrote no more sensation stories.

Even though she didn't write, she was very busy. It was a long and pleasant winter, and she didn't leave Mrs. Kirke till June.

She said good-bye to Mr. Bhaer warmly. "You won't forget to come and see us, now. I'll never forgive you if you forget, for I want my family to know my friend."

"Do you? Shall I come?" he asked eagerly.

"Yes, come next month. My best friend, Teddy, graduates then. I'm very proud of him." Something in Mr. Bhaer's face changed when her "best friend" was mentioned, and Jo blushed.

That night, after she had gone, he sat before his fire. "I must not hope it now," he said to himself with a sigh, but he was filled with longing.

Jo Burns Her Stories.

"I've Loved You Since I've Known You."

Chapter 18
Heartache

Laurie graduated with honor, and the whole March family and Mr. Laurence were very proud. But the look Laurie gave Jo after the ceremony made her think, "Oh dear! I know he'll say something, and then what shall I do?"

They met on a little path near the river. Dreadful pauses occurred in the conversation. But Jo saw that the moment had come.

"You've got to hear me out, Jo!" Laurie said. "I've loved you ever since I've known you. I've tried to show it, but you wouldn't let me."

"I wanted to save you this," she answered. "I never wanted you to care for me so. That's why I went away. I'm proud and fond of you, but I just can't love you as you want me to."

"Really, truly, Jo?" He took her hands.

"Oh, Teddy, I'm sorry. I can't help it. You know it's impossible for people to love other people if they don't." There was a long pause.

"Don't tell me, Jo, that you love that old man—that professor you were always writing about."

Jo wanted to laugh, but she said, "He isn't old. He's good and kind and the best friend I've got, next to you. I haven't the least idea of loving him or anyone else."

"But you will, and then what shall become of me?"

"You'll love someone else, too, and forget all this," she said sensibly.

Laurie threw himself on the ground, and it was very hard for Jo to continue. "You and I

Jo Tells Laurie the Truth.

are not suited to each other. We would be miserable if we married. So we'll be good friends all our lives. You'll see that I'm right by and by." He shook his head, but she went on. "You'll find some lovely girl. I'm homely and awkward and odd. I don't like elegant society and everything would be horrid! I don't believe I'll ever marry. I'm happy as I am and love my liberty too much."

"I know better!" broke in Laurie.

"I shall always be fond of you, but I'll never marry you!" cried Jo. At this, Laurie broke away, leaving Jo with her hands clasped tightly in her lap.

She went straight to Mr. Laurence and told him the dismal story. Laurie came home composed, went to his piano and played stormily, and then broke off.

"I can't stand this," said the old gentleman and told Laurie he knew. "Take it as a man and don't do anything rash. Why not go

Laurie Plays Stormily.

abroad, as you planned, and forget it?"

"Ah, but I didn't plan to go alone."

"I don't ask you to go alone. I am ready to go anywhere in the world with you."

Laurie hesitated. He knew his grandfather hated traveling. But before he had time to say anything, Mr. Laurence went on, "There is business in London that needs looking after. I've friends I will visit while you tour the continent."

Laurie sighed and then said, "As you like, sir. It doesn't matter where I go or what I do."

Soon they were off. Jo felt very guilty, but Laurie would allow no one to console him. When it came time for them to leave, he kissed each of the girls. Jo followed a minute after to wave a last good-bye. He left without a look behind him, and she knew the boy Laurie would never come back again.

Saying Good-Bye to Laurie

Beth Does Not Get Better.

Chapter 19
Beth's Secret

When Jo came home from Mrs. Kirke's that spring, she was struck with the change in Beth. A heavy weight fell on Jo when she saw her sister's face. It was thinner, and there was a strange transparent look about it.

When she proposed the trip to the mountains, Beth begged not to go so far from home. So Jo and Beth went to the seashore, where Beth could enjoy the open air and fresh sea breezes.

Jo wondered what Beth knew. One day she was looking at the thin cheeks and feeble

hands and felt that Beth was drifting away
Beth saw her looking and said, "Oh, Jo, yo
know now. I've known for a while, but
couldn't tell you. I'm never going to get well.

"Is this what made you so unhappy tha
you wouldn't let me comfort and help you?
Her heart ached to think of Beth learning t
say good-bye to health and love and life.

"It would have been selfish to frighte
you," said Beth.

"And I thought you were unhappy becaus
you loved Laurie," Jo confessed.

"How could I when he was so fond of you?
love him dearly, but he will never be any
thing to me but a brother," said Beth.

"Oh, Beth, you must get well. Nothing els
matters," Jo cried. And she held fast to Bet
as the sorrow crept over them.

Beth lay thinking a minute and then said
"I don't know how to say it, but I have a fee
ing that it was never intended I should liv

Sorrow Creeps Over the Girls.

long. I'm not like the rest of you. I never had any plans about what I'd do. I couldn't seem to imagine myself as anything but being Beth at home. I never wanted to go away, and the hard part now is leaving you all." Jo could not speak. "I only hope I see Amy again, but she seems so far away."

"She is coming in the spring, and I'm going to have you well and rosy by then," began Jo.

"Jo, don't hope any more. It won't do any good. We'll just enjoy being together now. You'll tell them at home, won't you?"

When they arrived home, there was no need for any words. Beth went right to bed. When Jo came downstairs, her father stood leaning his head on the mantelpiece, and her mother stretched out her arms to Jo for comfort.

No Need for Any Words

"I Thought You'd Never Come!"

Chapter 20
Lazy Laurence

Laurie was in Nice, France, on Christmas Day. A carriage with a single young lady stopped.

"Oh, Laurie, is it you? I thought you'd never come!" cried Amy, holding out both hands.

"I promised to spend Christmas with you, and here I am!"

"I have so much to say I don't know where to begin," said Amy excitedly.

Laurie got into the carriage and Amy watched him. She felt a new sort of shyness, for he was not the merry boy he had been. He was handsomer than ever, but he looked tired and unhappy.

"Beth is doing very poorly, Jo says," Amy began. "I often think I ought to go home."

"No, there's nothing you can do there," he said. Amy had Jo's letter out. Laurie took it, and smiling sadly, he put it in his pocket.

In the meantime, Laurie was also looking at Amy, who was as sprightly and graceful as ever.

Laurie had only intended to stay in Nice a week, but he stayed a month. He was tired of wandering around, and Amy reminded him of home.

Amy made a very good impression on Laurie, but she wondered what had happened to have changed him so.

"I am going out to sketch," said Amy as she joined Laurie one day. When she had settled herself, she asked, "Laurie, when are you going to your grandfather? He expects you,

Laurie Takes Jo's Letter.

and you really should go."

"I only bother him. So I thought I'd stay here and bother you a little longer," he said, lounging near her.

"What would Jo say if she saw you now?" said Amy, hoping to stir him.

"As usual, 'Go away, Teddy, I'm busy.'" He laughed, but it was harsh. Amy caught a new look on Laurie's face—a bitter look, full of pain and regret.

"You are so changed...." but there she stopped. "Well then, tell me what you've heard from home."

"I have nothing to tell."

"Don't you hear often? I thought Jo would write a lot," she said.

Amy did not like him this new way, so she launched into a speech: "I have a new name for you. It's Lazy Laurence. How do you like it?" Her voice was sharp.

"That's not bad."

Lazy Laurence

"Do you want to know what I think of you?" she continued. "Well, I despise you."

Laurie was taken aback. "Why?" he asked.

"Instead of being good, useful and happy, you're lazy and miserable. You have been abroad six months and have done nothing but waste time and disappoint your friends. You are much worse since you left home."

The lecture had some effect, for Laurie's eyes sparkled, he sat up, and held out his hand.

Then Amy noticed that he wore the small ring Jo had given him long ago, and she suddenly knew. Laurie never spoke of Jo. She recalled the shadow that had passed over his face a moment ago. Amy had thought that maybe love was the cause of his problems, but now she was sure.

"Laurie," she began in her sweetest voice, "they ought to have told me. Did that girl you liked, Miss Randall, break—"

Amy Lectures Laurie.

"No, it wasn't her. You know perfectly well I never cared for anyone but Jo," said Laurie, turning his face away. "If I'm a good-for-nothing, it's her fault, and you may tell her."

"I'm sorry, Teddy dear—"

"Don't! That's her name for me." He pulled at the grass. Presently he said, "Do you think Jo would despise me as you do?"

"Yes, if she saw you now. She hates lazy people. If you'd set upon a task, you'd soon be your happy, hearty self again."

"That's impossible!"

"Try it and see" was Amy's advice.

Neither spoke for several minutes, and Amy felt a shade of coldness in his manner, but was glad she had said what she did.

Next morning, instead of his usual call, she found a note. It said that "Lazy Laurence" had gone to his grandpa.

"I'm glad he's gone," said Amy, but added with a sigh, "I shall miss him."

A Note for Amy

A Pleasant Room for Beth

Chapter 21
The Valley of the Shadow

The family accepted that Beth was not going to get well. They tried to bear it cheerfully.

The most pleasant room in the house was set apart for Beth, and in it they gathered everything she most loved. Nothing changed her nature, and the first few months were happy ones.

But by and by, Beth said her needle was "so heavy" and she put it down. Talking wearied her. Long nights followed heavy days.

Jo never left her for an hour. She slept on

a couch in the room. Often when she woke, she found Beth reading or singing softly while slow tears dropped through her fingers.

One night Beth looked among the books on her table and found a little paper scribbled in Jo's hand. It was a poem about her. Beth's one regret was that she had done so little, but the poem seemed to assure her that her life had not been useless.

When Jo came to her bedside, Beth said, "It's such a comfort to know that someone loves me as much as you do. You must take my place, Jo, and be everything to Mother and Father when I'm gone."

The spring days came, and the birds came back to say good-bye to Beth. In the dark hour before the dawn, she drew her last breath with one loving look, one sigh.

When morning came, for the first time in many months, the fire was out and Beth's room was empty.

A Dark Hour

Thoughts of Amy

Chapter 22
Learning to Forget

Laurie kept remembering Amy's words: "Go and do something splendid that will make her love you." Mr. Laurence noted a change, and Laurie admitted he had been selfish and lazy.

He decided to put his sorrow in love into music, but instead caught himself humming dancing tunes from the Christmas ball he had gone to with Amy. He knew a change was going on in spite of himself.

Laurie thought that forgetting Jo would take years, but to his great surprise, it grew easier every day. His love for Jo slowly changed to tender affection. He received a letter from her saying that Beth was worse and telling him to write Amy often so she would not feel lonely or homesick.

So he did write to Amy, but he also took off Jo's little ring from his finger and locked it in the drawer with her letters.

Amy answered Laurie's letter right away, and letters flew back and forth between them. He wanted to see her, but she didn't ask him. She grew pale and thoughtful.

While these changes were going on abroad, trouble had come at home. The sad news of Beth's death met Amy at Vevay, in Switzerland. She bore it very well, but her heart was heavy, and she longed to be at home. Laurie was in Germany when he heard the news, and he set off immediately to comfort Amy.

He knew Vevay well and hurried to Amy. She was sitting in the garden, thinking of

Laurie Rushes to Comfort Amy.

Beth and wondering why Laurie didn't come.
She did not hear him cross the courtyard, but
the minute she looked up she ran to him saying, "Oh, Laurie, I knew you'd come to me!"

Amy felt no one could comfort her as well
as Laurie, and Laurie decided that Amy was
the only woman in the world who could fill
Jo's place. For an hour they walked and
talked, and Amy felt her loneliness and sorrow lift.

The moment Aunt Carrol saw Amy's face
she thought, "Now I understand—the child
has been pining for young Laurence."

The Swiss air did them both good, and in
spite of the sorrow, it was a happy time.

There was no need for Laurie to tell Amy
he loved her. She knew it without words.

While rowing on the lake one day, he
asked her if she would be his, and she answered, "Yes, Laurie."

A Marriage Proposal

Dark Days for Jo

Chapter 23
All Alone

These were dark days for Jo, and she was filled with despair at the thought of spending all her days in that quiet house. Often she started up at night, thinking Beth had called, but her mother came to comfort her, and her father was there in the study when she wanted to talk.

As they sat sewing, she saw how happy her sister Meg was. Jo loved the babies tenderly, and Meg saw a glimmer of Jo's old spirit when they were around.

"Why don't you write? That always used to

make you happy," said her mother one day.

"I've no heart to write," answered Jo. "Nobody cares for my things anyway."

"We do," said her mother. "Write something for us. I'm sure it would do you good."

An hour afterward, her mother peeped in and found Jo scratching away. Her father sent Jo's story—much against her will—to a magazine, which paid for it and requested others. For a small thing, it was a great success. So Jo wrote more stories.

When Amy and Laurie wrote of their engagement, Mrs. March feared Jo would not be able to rejoice over it. Though Jo looked grave at first, she was full of hopes for "the children." Mrs. March said she had suspected it all along, but hadn't wanted to suggest to Jo that her Teddy loved someone else. "Forgive me, dear," Mrs. March added, "I can't help seeing that you are lonely, and I wondered if he came back and asked again if you

Jo Tries Writing Again.

might give a different answer."

"No, Mother," said Jo. But she went back and read the letter again and sighed, "How very happy they must be."

Then she went up to her garret and cried, wondering why one sister should have all she asked, and the other nothing. She drew out some notebooks she had written at Mrs. Kirke's, and her eye caught on a little message written in Professor Bhaer's hand.

"Oh, how I should love to see him. My dear Friedrich, I didn't value him half enough when I had him."

One evening Jo was alone on the sofa thinking. Her face looked tired and grave. She had fallen asleep and was awakened by Laurie as he stooped down to kiss her. She flew up crying, "Oh, my Teddy!"

"Dear Jo, are you glad to see me?"

"Oh, yes, and where's Amy?"

Jo Longs to See Her Friend.

"Your mother has got my wife down at Meg's," Laurie replied.

"Your *what*?" cried Jo. "You've gone and got married!"

"Yes," he said, going on his knees, "the one and only time! I wanted to be the one to tell you."

"Why didn't you let us know?"

"We wanted to surprise everyone!" he said, and then they settled down for a good talk, for Jo wanted to hear the whole story. Laurie then took her hand and said, "Jo, dear, I want to say one thing, and then we'll put it aside forever. I shall never stop loving you, but the love is changed. I was a boy when I first loved you, and I made a fool of myself. But will you now go back to the happy old times we used to have?"

"We can't go back and mustn't expect to. I see the change in you, and you'll find it in me. But we will be brother and sister, and

A Great Surprise!

help one another all our lives."

Jo didn't want the homecoming to be sad, but Laurie said, "Poor Jo, we left you to bear it alone. You *are* older, and your eyes are sad. You've had a great deal to bear."

"No, I had help. I am lonely sometimes, but—"

"You shall never be again," broke in Laurie. "Amy and I can't get on without you, and we'll all be happy and friendly together."

But then Amy's voice was heard calling, "Where is she? Where is my dear old Jo?"

In trooped the whole family, and everyone was hugged and kissed all over again. Amy's face was full of brightness, and everyone made much of the three travelers, for they had been gone three years. They had tea, and then everyone went upstairs except Jo, who felt a sudden sense of loneliness come over her. For even her Teddy had deserted her.

But then there came a knock at the door.

All Together Again

She opened it and started as if another ghost had come to surprise her. There stood a tall bearded gentleman.

"Oh, Mr. Bhaer, I am so glad to see you," cried Jo, clutching him.

"And I to see Miss March."

"Come in, my sister and friends have just come home, and we are all very happy." She couldn't hide her joy at seeing him, and the welcome gave him hope.

"Have you been ill, my friend?" he asked abruptly, for the light fell on Jo's face, and he saw a change in it.

"Not ill, but tired and sorrowful."

"Ah, yes, I know. I heard." They shook hands again, and Jo felt comforted.

Mr. Bhaer received a warm welcome upstairs. The twins went to him at once, and the women looked on with approval. Laurie stood aloof, feeling a twinge—not of jealousy, but of suspicion—but it did not last long.

Another Surprise

Mr. Bhaer's face looked alive with interest, actually young and handsome, Jo thought. He was dressed in a new black suit. Nothing about him escaped Jo, who sat knitting away quietly. "Dear old fellow! He couldn't have got himself up better if he'd been going courting," said Jo to herself, and then she blushed at her thought.

Everyone sat around the fire talking until Meg finally made a move to go. "We must have our sing, for we are all together again," said Jo. But even though they were not *all* there, Beth still seemed among them.

"I too shall go," Mr. Bhaer said, "but I will gladly come again, for a little business will keep me in the city a few days." He spoke to Mrs. March, but looked at Jo.

Jo wondered what business had brought Mr. Bhaer to the city. She would have known if she could have seen how, later in his room, he looked at a picture of her.

Mr. Bhaer Has Come "On Business."

Caught in the Rain

Chapter 24
Under the Umbrella

By the second week Mr. Bhaer was there, everyone knew perfectly well what was going on. The Professor's hat was on the March's hall table nearly every evening, and Jo sang as she went about her work and did up her hair four times a day.

But then Mr. Bhaer stayed away for three days. Jo was very cross as she set out for her daily walk one dull afternoon. She went the long way and soon felt a drop of rain on her cheek. "It serves me right," she said to herself as she got wetter, "to put on my best things and wander about, hoping to see the Professor." She was rushing across the street when she heard a voice:

"You have no umbrella!" Mr. Bhaer smiled and held his over her head.

"We thought you had gone," said Jo hastily, trying to keep her voice calm.

"Do you think I would go without saying good-bye to those who have been so kind? No, I will come one more time before I go."

"You *are* going then?"

"I no longer have any business here. My friends have found a place for me at a college, where I will teach as I did in Germany."

"How splendid!" cried Jo.

"Ah, but I fear this place is not near here. It is in the west."

"So far away!" said Jo, her face falling.

Mr. Bhaer grew more hopeful at her exclamation. Walking home, Jo's feet were cold, but her heart felt colder. Mr. Bhaer was

Mr. Bhaer Holds the Umbrella.

going away, he only cared for her as a friend. A few tears fell from her eyes.

Mr. Bhaer saw them and asked, "Dearest heart, why do you cry?"

"Because you are going away," Jo answered in a most undignified way.

"Jo," cried Mr. Bhaer, clasping his hands, "I came to see if you could care for me. I wanted to be sure I was more than a friend. Am I?"

"Oh, yes!" said Jo happily. "Friedrich," she added bashfully, "why didn't you tell me sooner?"

"I had a wish to tell you when I said good-bye in New York, but I thought you were in love with your handsome friend."

"Teddy was only a boy and soon got over his little fancy," said Jo. "But I don't know if I would have said yes then. You came just when I wanted you."

"Although my heart is full, I cannot take

More Than a Friend

you from your happy home till I have one to give you. Have you patience? I must go away and do my work alone and care for my nephews. Can you be happy while we hope and wait?"

"Yes, I can, for we love one another." Then Jo, who never would learn to be proper, kissed her Friedrich under the umbrella.

For a year Jo and her professor worked and waited, met occasionally, and wrote many long letters.

In the beginning of the second year, Aunt March died, and she left her large house to Jo. She and Friedrich decided to open a school for boys.

"I've always longed for boys, and now I can fill a whole house with them! Friedrich will teach, and Father will help too. And we'll all help with the work."

Almost before she knew where she was, Jo found herself married and settled. The school flourished and was filled with poor boys as

A School Filled with Boys

well as rich.

It was hard work, and they never became rich from it. Jo was a happy woman in spite of the work and the constant racket. As the years went on, she had two little lads of her own—Rob, named for Grandpa, and Teddy, a happy-go-lucky baby with his father's sun-shiny disposition.

Five years after Jo's wedding, the Marches, the Brookes, the Laurences and the Bhaers all gathered in the orchard for apple-picking. Meg, Jo and Amy sat under the tree with their mother, thinking about the life they had pictured for themselves long ago. Then Mrs. March stretched out her arms, gathering her children to her. She smiled and said:

"Oh, my girls, however long you live, I never can wish you a greater happiness than this."

No Greater Happiness Than This

HEIDI
Johanna Spyri

Contents

About the Author

Johanna Spyri was born in 1829 in the Swiss village of Hirzel. Her house overlooked the mountains, and they inspired her to write the story of *Heidi*.

Johanna Spyri moved to the city of Zurich after she married an attorney. Her yearning for her childhood home in the small village came out in the many children's stories she wrote.

Although the author died in 1901, *Heidi* lives on as a story about the joy of life in the Swiss Alps.

A Footpath Winds up the Mountain.

Chapter 1
The Journey up the Mountain

The Swiss town of Mayenfeld lies at the foot of a mountain range whose rugged peaks tower high above the valley below. Behind the town a footpath winds gently up the mountain.

One sunny June morning, a tall, strong woman was climbing up the path. She had a bundle in one hand and held a little girl about five years old by the other hand. The child's cheeks were flushed and sunburned, and she was wearing two dresses, one on top of the other. She looked like a shapeless bundle of clothing trudging uphill on a pair of shoes.

After climbing for almost an hour, they reached a little village called Dorfli. This was where the woman used to live, and the people of the town remembered her and called to her from their houses. She did not answer, but continued on her way until she reached a house at the very end of the main street. There a voice from inside called to her:

"Half a minute, Detie, and I'll come with you if you're going any farther."

Detie stood still, but the little girl sat down on the ground.

"Tired, Heidi?" Detie asked her.

"No, but I'm very hot," the child answered.

"We'll be there soon. Just keep going, and we'll be there in an hour."

At that moment a plump, pleasant-faced woman came out of the house and joined them. The little girl got up and followed as

Climbing Up the Path

the two grown-ups went ahead, gossiping about people who lived in Dorfli or around it.

The woman finally asked Detie where she was going with Heidi. Detie explained that when her sister died a few years ago, Heidi was all alone in the world. So Detie had taken her in and raised her. But now she had been offered a wonderful job in a good family, but the family lived in a city far away.

"Well then, who will take care of poor Heidi now?" asked the woman.

"I am taking her up to Uncle Alp who lives on the mountain. It's high time he took some responsibility for her. After all, he is her grandfather."

The woman looked shocked. Everyone knew that Uncle Alp was strange. He lived all alone on a mountain. He never talked to anyone in the village, and he hadn't set foot in church for years. He had a wild look in his eyes, and he wore a long white beard. No one

Detie's Friend Joins Her.

really knew how he got the name "Uncle
Alp" or why he had lived alone for so many
years.

But Detie's friend felt sure that Detie knew
more about the old man than anyone else.
After coaxing her friend for a little while, the
woman got Detie to tell her this story:

"Uncle Alp grew up in a fine house in a
lovely village. He was the oldest son and had
only one younger brother. Instead of living a
quiet life in the village, Uncle Alp longed for
the exciting life in the city. He traveled all
over, got into bad company, and drank and
gambled away all his property. His poor parents died of shame and grief when they
heard of it. His brother was ruined too. He
ran away somewhere, and no one heard of
him again.

"Uncle Alp disappeared too. He had nothing left but a bad name. He was finally discovered in the army in a country far away.

Uncle Alp's Fine House

Then no one heard of him for twelve or fifteen years. One day he reappeared in the village with a young son and asked some of his relatives to look after the boy, but everyone refused. No one wanted anything to do with him or the boy. He was so angry that he vowed he would never set foot in the village again. So he came to Dorfli and settled down there with the boy, whose name was Tobias. No one ever knew what had happened to his wife. Most people believed that she died.

"Anyway, he saved a little money and apprenticed his son to a carpenter. Everyone learned to like the boy, but no one trusted the old man! There were all sorts of rumors about him deserting the army to avoid some trouble he had gotten into.

"All the same, he was accepted as a member of the family. His grandmother and my grandmother were sisters, so we called him Uncle, and since we're related to almost

Uncle Alp Reappeared with a Young Boy.

everyone in Dorfli, the whole village soon called him Uncle too. Then when he went to live on the mountain it became Uncle Alp!

"Anyway, after Tobias learned his trade, he came home to Dorfli and married my sister. They settled down very happily together. But only two years later, he was killed by a falling beam while he was building a house. My poor sister went into such a shock that she fell ill with a fever and never walked again. She only lived for a few more weeks. Everyone said the tragedy was Uncle's punishment for his own mistakes. They told him to his face that he was to blame, and even the pastor told him to do penance to clear his conscience. That made him so angry that he refused to speak to anyone. He went up on the mountain to live and hasn't been down since. My mother and I took my sister's child, Heidi, to live with us. But now I must go away, and there is no one but Uncle Alp to

Uncle Alp Refused to Speak.

take care of her."

Detie's friend looked at her with disapproval. She even told Detie that she was surprised that Detie could hand Heidi over to the old man just like that. But Detie said that she had no choice and continued on her way up the mountain.

Continuing up the Mountain

Peter the Goatherd

Chapter 2
Peter the Goatherd

While Detie was telling her friend all about Uncle Alp, Heidi had become friends with a young boy named Peter. Peter was eleven, and every morning he went down to Dorfli to gather the goats and drive them up to graze in the mountain meadows. Then, in the evening, he brought them down again.

The summer was the only time when Peter could see other boys and girls. For the rest of the time, goats were his only companions. He spent very little time at home with his mother and his old, blind grandmother who lived with them. He left the hut very early and always stayed as long as possible with the children in Dorfli. His father had been the goatherd before him, but he had been killed several years ago while chopping down a tall tree. His mother's name was Bridget, but everyone just called her "the goatherd's mother." Everyone called his grandmother "Grannie."

Now Heidi and Peter were running and playing in the fresh grass on the side of the mountain. Heidi had removed some of her heavy clothing, and when Detie caught up with the two children she scolded Heidi and made her wrap the discarded clothing in a bundle. Peter followed along and carried the bundle for Heidi.

When they finally reached the top of the mountain, there was Uncle Alp, sitting peacefully with his pipe in his mouth and his hands on his knees. Peter and Heidi had run

Running in the Fresh Grass

ahead of Detie. Heidi was the first to reach the old man. She went straight up to him and held out her hand.

"Hello, Grandfather," she said.

"Hey, what's that?" he exclaimed gruffly as he took her hand. She stared at the old man. She was fascinated by his long beard and bushy grey eyebrows. Meanwhile, Detie came towards them while Peter stood and watched to see what would happen.

"Good morning, Uncle," said Detie. "I have brought you Tobias' daughter. I don't suppose you recognize her, since you haven't seen her since she was a year old."

"Why have you brought her here?" he demanded roughly. "And you be off with your goats," he said to Peter. The old man gave him such a look that Peter disappeared at once.

Detie explained to her uncle that Heidi was his responsibility now. She reminded

"Hello, Grandfather."

him that he was the child's closest relative and that he would have to answer for it if any harm came to her.

Uncle Alp got angry at Detie's warning.

"Go back where you came from and don't come here again," he said angrily, raising his arm.

Detie didn't wait to be told twice. She said good-bye to Heidi and ran down the mountain, not stopping till she reached Dorfli.

Detie Runs down the Mountain.

The Old Man Stares at the Ground.

Chapter 3
At Grandfather's

As soon as Detie left, the old man went inside and sat down again. He stared at the ground in silence, blowing great clouds of smoke from his pipe, while Heidi explored her new home.

After she had looked around for a while, she asked the old man to show her what was inside the hut. She picked up her bundle of clothes to take with her. The inside was one large room. There was a table and a chair and a bed in one corner. Opposite that was a stove. There was a door in one wall which the old man opened, and she saw it was a large closet.

"Where will I sleep, Grandfather" asked Heidi.

"Wherever you like," he answered.

This answer pleased Heidi, and she soon discovered a ladder which led to a hayloft. Heidi loved the sweet-smelling hay and decided to make her bed right there in the loft. Grandfather smiled when he saw Heidi so happy. He brought her a pillow, sheets, a warm blanket, and a thick cloth which they used to make a mattress. Heidi was so pleased with her new bed that she could hardly wait to go to sleep. But her grandfather reminded her that she still had not eaten her dinner. So he went to the big stove and prepared a simple but hearty meal for both of them. When Grandfather was finished cooking, Heidi went to the closet and found plates and silverware on a shelf. She set the table,

The Ladder to the Hayloft

and her grandfather smiled and praised her for being so helpful.

Not long after finishing her meal, Heidi became sleepy, for she had had an exciting day. She said good night to her grandfather and climbed into her bed in the hayloft.

During the night the wind blew so hard that it shook the whole hut and made its beams creak. It shrieked down the chimney and brought one or two of the old fir tree branches crashing down. The old man became worried. He thought that Heidi would be frightened. He climbed up the ladder and went to her bed. The moonlight shone through a small opening in the roof, and he could see Heidi's face. She was fast asleep under the heavy blanket. Her cheek was resting on her chubby little arm, and she had a wonderful, happy expression on her face. The old man stood looking at her until the clouds covered the moon and darkened the room.

The Moon Shines on Heidi's Face.

Happy in Her New Life

Chapter 4
A Visit to Grannie

All through that summer Heidi went up to
the pasture every day with her friend Peter
and his goats. She grew tanned and happy in
her new life. She loved her old grandfather,
and life on the mountain made her feel as
free as the birds that sang in the big fir trees
near the hut. But when autumn came, strong
winds began to blow and Grandfather said:

"Today you must stay at home. A little
girl like you might get blown over the side
of the mountain by a gust of wind."

Peter was disappointed when Heidi could

275

not go with him. He had grown used to her company, and he found it lonely and dull to be without her. The goats were twice as troublesome when she was not there. They seemed to miss her and scattered all over the place, as though they were looking for her.

But Heidi managed to be happy wherever she was. She enjoyed staying at the hut and watching her grandfather at his carpentry and his other jobs.

Then all at once it turned really cold, and Peter arrived in the mornings blowing on his hands to warm them. One night it started to snow. It, snowed until there was not a single leaf to be seen. Heidi watched from the window. She loved the thick white snow and hoped it would go on falling until the hut was buried up to the window sills, so it would be impossible to go out. But that did not happen, and the next morning Grandfather was able to dig his way out and clear a path to

Heidi Watches Grandfather.

the hut. No sooner was the path clear, than Peter came for a visit. He came in and sat by the fire while Grandfather asked him about school.

In the winter Peter went to school to learn to read and write. Immediately Heidi wanted to know just what he did at school. She had so many questions that even Grandfather began to laugh as Peter tried to answer them as fast as Heidi thought them up.

After Heidi was satisfied, Grandfather made dinner. When Peter was finished, he thanked the old man an invited both of them to come and visit his grannie. Heidi was delighted at the idea of going to visit someone, so the very next morning she asked her grandfather to take her there. But Uncle Alp tried to put her off by saying that the snow was too deep.

But the idea of visiting Grannie was firmly in her head, and day after day she mentioned

Peter Tells Heidi about School.

HEIDI

her wish to visit the old woman to Grandfather. Finally, one morning, Grandfather dragged a big sleigh out of the shed. It had a bar along one side to hold on to and a big steering wheel. They went down the mountain so fast that Heidi felt as though she was flying. She screamed with delight. They stopped with a jerk just outside Peter's hut. Grandfather told her to go in, and he turned up the mountain, pulling the sleigh behind him.

The door Heidi opened led into a small kitchen in which there was a stove and some pots on a shelf. A door led into another small room, which had a low ceiling and was very cramped. In the second room Heidi saw two women. One was mending a jacket and the other one, who was old and bent, sat in a corner. Heidi went straight to the old woman and said:

"Hello, Grannie. Here I am at last."

Grandfather Drags Out a Big Sleigh.

HEIDI

Grannie raised her head and felt for Heidi's hand. Then she said, "Are you the child from Uncle Alp's?" The two women were surprised when Heidi told them that her grandfather had wrapped her up in a warm blanket and brought her down for a visit.

Heidi looked about the room while the women were talking, and she missed nothing.

"One of your shutters is hanging loose, Grannie," she said. "Grandfather will fix it. It will break the window if nothing is done. Look how it bangs to and fro."

"I can't see it, my dear," answered Grannie, "but I can hear it and everything else that cracks and clatters in here. The place is falling apart, and at night I am afraid that sometime it may fall on us and kill us all. And there's no one to do anything about it."

Heidi looked at the old woman.

"Why can't you see the shutter?" she asked. The old woman tried to explain that she

Grannie Feels for Heidi's Hand.

was blind, but Heidi did not understand. She took Grannie's hand and led her to the window so she could look out at the falling snow. The old woman tried again to explain, but Heidi was persistent.

"Even in summer, Grannie? Surely you can see the sunshine and watch it sink behind the mountains and make them all red like fire. Can't you?"

When Grannie sadly shook her head, it was more than Heidi could bear, and she began to cry. She wished she could help Grannie, but there was nothing she or anyone else could do. The old woman tried to comfort the little girl, and she told her that as long as she came to visit, being blind wasn't half so bad. Heidi promised to return very soon and to bring her grandfather along to fix the broken shutter. The women looked at her in disbelief, for the old man hadn't come down to the bottom of the mountain in many years.

The Falling Snow

HEIDI

But after her visit, Uncle Alp was waiting outside to bring Heidi back up the mountain. On the way up, Heidi told him about Grannie and the broken shutter and the little hut that needed so many repairs. The old man did not seem interested in fixing anything for the women, but when Heidi told him how much it meant to her, he agreed.

The very next morning, Heidi and her grandfather appeared at the little hut. Heidi ran in and kissed Peter's mother and Grannie. Soon they heard the sound of a hammer on the outside of the hut. Bridget, Peter's mother, ran outside to see Uncle Alp making all the repairs. She invited him in, but he only said no and kept on hammering.

Uncle Alp Repairs the Hut.

Content in Her Mountain Home

Chapter 5
Two Unexpected Visitors

A winter passed and then another summer, and Heidi's second winter on the mountain was nearly over. She was now seven and had learned many useful things from her grandfather. She visited Peter's mother and Grannie every week and had come to love both women very much. Heidi felt content and peaceful in her mountain home.

Twice during the winter Peter had brought up messages from the schoolmaster in Dorfli to say that Uncle Alp must send Heidi to school. But the old man refused to answer the

notes and told Peter that he had no inten
tion of sending Heidi to school.

One March morning, just when the su
began to melt the snow on the slopes, Heid
saw an old man standing outside the hut. H
was dressed in black and looked very solemn
He looked at her and said:

"Don't be afraid of me. I'm fond of childrer
Come and shake hands. You must be Heid
and where is your grandfather?"

"He's indoors making wooden spoons," sh
told him and showed him in.

He was the old pastor from Dorfli, who ha
been a neighbor of Uncle Alp's when he ha
lived there. He came to tell Uncle Alp that :
was time that Heidi went to school. But th
old man insisted that Heidi would be bette
off living on the mountain and learning an
growing with the birds and the animal:
instead of going off to school where she migh
learn bad ways. But the pastor insisted tha

The Pastor from Dorfli

HEIDI

Uncle Alp return to the village so that Heidi would be able to begin school in the winter. Uncle Alp shook the pastor's hand but said slowly:

"I know what you mean about the child going to school, but I can't do what you ask. That's final. I won't send her to school or come back to the village to live."

The pastor shook his head sadly and walked slowly down the hill. All this left Uncle Alp in a bad mood, and he hardly said a word to Heidi all day.

The next morning, while the old man was still his bad mood, there came a knock at the door. This time it was Detie. She was wearing a hat with a feather and a long dress which swept the ground as she walked. Uncle Alp looked her up and down in silence.

"How well Heidi looks," she said. "I hardly recognize her. Of course I have been meaning to come back for her, but for two years I have

Another Visitor—Detie

HEIDI

been just so busy I haven't had a chance to return!"

Then Detie went on to explain that all the time she had been away she was looking for a proper home for Heidi. Now she had finally found one. There was a rich family who lived in the city. They had a young daughter who was paralyzed and had to spend all her time sitting in a wheelchair. The girl was very lonely, and the family had been looking for a playmate and companion for her. So Detie immediately thought of Heidi and came straightaway to bring her back to the city.

The old man said that he wouldn't part with the child, but that did not stop Detie. She became quite angry with Uncle Alp and told him how she had heard in the village about his refusal to send Heidi to school. She threatened to take him to court if she was stopped from taking Heidi with her. The old man got very angry.

Grandfather Is Very Angry.

HEIDI

"That's enough!" he thundered. "Take her then and spoil her. But don't ever bring her back to me. I don't want to see her with a feather in her hat or hear her talk to me as you have done today." Then he strode away.

Heidi looked very unhappy and went to run after the old man. Detie grabbed her and told her to pack her clothes and prepare to leave. Heidi refused. But Detie told the child that the old man wanted her to leave for the city. When Heidi still refused to go, Detie promised her that she could buy a nice present for Grannie and return to the mountain whenever she wanted to. This sounded better to Heidi, and she daydreamed about surprising Grannie with some soft white rolls from the city.

Heidi Leaves with Detie.

A Fashionable House in the City

Chapter 6
A New Life Begins

The house in the city to which Heidi was being taken belonged to a wealthy man called Mr. Seseman. His only daughter, Clara, was an invalid and spent all her days in a wheelchair. She was a very patient child, with a thin, pale face and mild blue eyes. Her mother had died many years ago, so her father had hired a housekeeper to take care of the little girl. The housekeeper's name was Miss Rottenmeier. She was a capable woman, but she was very strict and never laughed or even smiled. Since Mr. Seseman was so wealthy he also hired two servants, Sebastian and Tinette, to take care of the big house.

When Heidi and Detie arrived at the house, Clara was sitting up in her wheelchair expecting them. They stood in the doorway and waited for Miss Rottenmeier to invite them inside.

Miss Rottenmeier led them into the large sitting room and looked Heidi up and down. She did not like what she saw. Heidi was wearing a shabby cotton dress, which was the only kind she had.

"What's your name?" asked Miss Rottenmeier.

When Heidi answered, the housekeeper looked astonished.

"That can't be your *real* name!" she said.

But before Heidi had a chance to answer, Detie interrupted and explained to the woman that Heidi was shy and had never been in the city before and that her real

Clara

name was Adelheid, after her mother. Miss Rottenmeier continued to question Heidi, and when she found out that Heidi could neither read nor write, she became quite upset. She did not think that this shabby little girl from the mountains would be a fit companion for Clara. But Detie would hear none of it and quickly left the house, promising to return if things did not go well.

All this time Heidi had not moved, not even when Detie left her. Clara, who had watched everything from her wheelchair, now called her over.

"Do you want to be called Heidi or Adelheid?" she asked.

"Everyone calls me Heidi. That's my name," she answered.

In a short time, Clara and Heidi got to know each other. Clara explained that her life was lonely and dull. She had only her tutor, Mr. Usher, to keep her company. But

Miss Rottenmeier Questions Heidi.

now she had Heidi, and she was looking forward to having a friend. Before Heidi had time to answer and to tell Clara that she would be returning soon to her grandfather, Peter and Grannie, Miss Rottenmeier walked into the room and announced that dinner would be served.

The dining room was the biggest room Heidi had ever seen. Beside Heidi's plate lay a nice white roll, and her eyes lit up at the sight of it. She knew Grannie would love this soft bread. When Sebastian offered her a dish of baked fish, Heidi asked if she could have the roll. Sebastian nodded. When Heidi picked up the roll and put it in her pocket, he could hardly keep a straight face.

Then Heidi tried to talk to Sebastian, and Miss Rottenmeier began a long lecture on table manners and why she should never talk to the servants during dinner. When she was quite through, she turned to Heidi only to

The Biggest Room Heidi Has Ever Seen

discover that the child, who had had a long day, was fast asleep.

Sebastian carried the sleeping Heidi up the winding staircase to a beautiful room. She opened her eyes just long enough to see a bed such as she had never seen before. There were lovely soft sheets and four plump pillows at the head of the bed. As soon as her head touched the pillow, Heidi was asleep again.

Sebastian Carries the Sleeping Heidi.

Heavy Curtains

Chapter 7
A Bad Day for Miss Rottenmeier

Heidi awoke the next morning and looked around her. She forgot where she was and rubbed her eyes a few times until she remembered that she was no longer in the hut with her grandfather.

She jumped out of bed and dressed quickly. She went first to one window, then to the other, and tried to pull back the curtains so that she could see what was outside. The curtains were so heavy that she could only pull them a little bit away from the window. But still, all she could see were walls and

HEIDI

windows. She began to feel frightened. At Grandfather's she had always gone out of doors first thing in the morning to see the sky, trees and flowers. Heidi felt trapped in the house, and she could not understand what life in the city could be like.

Just then, there was a tap at the door, and Tinette, one of the servants, announced that breakfast was ready. Heidi really had no idea what breakfast was, since Grandfather had never announced meals in so formal a way. So she got in the bed in her room and waited. After a while Miss Rottenmeier came up and scolded Heidi for being late and led her downstairs to the dining room.

After the meal, Heidi found herself alone with Clara. Soon Heidi was chatting about her life at home with Grandfather and all the things she loved so much on the mountain. While they were talking, Mr. Usher, the tutor, arrived. Miss Rottenmeier took him

Heidi Waits in Her Room.

aside and explained that Heidi was with Clara. She told Mr. Usher that the child could neither read nor write, and that she feared she could never learn. But Mr. Usher was a fair man, and he said he would like to meet the child and see for himself. So Miss Rottenmeier led him into the study, and she went into another room.

Suddenly, there was a tremendous clatter in the study, as though a lot of things had fallen down. Miss Rottenmeier hurried into the room and found the floor strewn with books, paper and ink. Heidi was nowhere to be seen. Mr. Usher explained that Heidi had just rushed across the room, caught the table-cloth as she went by, and swept everything onto the floor with it. Miss Rottenmeier was very angry, and she hurried off to find Heidi. She finally found her standing by the open door, looking up and down the street with a puzzled expression on her face. Heidi thought

Mr. Usher Wants to Judge for Himself.

she had heard the rustling of fir trees, but it had only been the sound of a carriage moving over the cobblestone streets. Miss Rottenmeier was very angry, and she made Heidi promise that she would sit still in her chair during her lessons and never again run from the room. Heidi accepted this as one more rule she had to obey.

After Tinette cleaned up the room, Mr. Usher left and Clara went to take a nap. Heidi did not have anything to do, so she asked Sebastian if he could open one of the big, heavy windows. He helped her up on a stool so she could look outside. But all Heidi could see were buildings and stony streets. She asked Sebastian where she could go to see the whole valley. He answered that she would have to go high up in the church tower to get a view of the entire city.

Heidi climbed down from the stool and ran downstairs and out the front door. But she

Down the Big Stairs

could not seem to find the tower. She walked down many winding streets and passed many people, but they all seemed in such a hurry that she did not dare stop them to ask directions.

Finally she saw a boy standing at a corner. He held a small tambourine in one hand and a large tortoise in the other. Heidi went up to him and asked him how she might find the church tower. He said he would take her there, but that it would cost her a quarter. She thought for a minute and then told him that she hadn't any money, but that Clara did and would be happy to give it to him. So the boy led Heidi through the winding streets.

When they finally reached the church, an old man opened the door for them. Heidi explained that she wanted to see the view from the tower. The old man scratched his head but showed her the way up to the tower

A Boy with a Tambourine and a Tortoise

anyway. But when Heidi looked out, all she could see was a sea of roofs, chimneys and towers. Heidi was so disappointed that the old man decided to try and cheer her up.

"Come and look at our kittens," he said. "Maybe you would like one."

When Heidi saw the furry little creatures she cried with delight. She could hardly believe her ears when she heard the old man say that she could have some of her very own. She chose an all-white kitten and a brown one, and put one in each pocket. Then she said good bye to the old man and told him that there was plenty of room in the big house for the rest of the kittens. He asked her where she lived and promised to bring the rest if he couldn't find homes for them. Then Heidi asked the boy to help her find her way back home.

Soon they reached the house. Heidi pulled the bell and Sebastian came to the door. He

Furry Little Kittens

was very worried and asked Heidi where she had been.

When Heidi went into the dining room, there was an awful silence. Miss Rottenmeier looked very cross and said:

"It was extremely naughty of you to leave the house without asking permission or saying a word to anyone, and then to go roaming about until this late hour. I've never heard of such a thing."

"Meow," came the reply.

"How dare you make fun of me!" shouted Miss Rottenmeier.

But before Heidi could answer, the kittens began meowing again. Miss Rottenmeier got so angry that she stood up and started to shake her finger at Heidi, when the two kittens fell out of Heidi's pockets.

"What! Kittens here?" screamed Miss Rottenmeier. And she rushed out of the room, calling for Sebastian. She called for him to

"What! Kittens Here?"

get rid of the kittens at once.

Sebastian was laughing so hard that he had to wait outside the door to compose himself before he could come in. But now Clara had the kittens on her lap and was delighted with them.

"Sebastian, you must help us," said Clara. "Find a corner where Miss Rottenmeier won't look and hide the kittens there. She will certainly get rid of them if she sees them, but we want to have them to play with when we're alone."

Sebastian smiled and said he had just the place for them. He could tell that with Heidi around there would be even more excitement in the future, and he always enjoyed seeing prissy Miss Rottenmeier in a rage.

Sebastian Laughs Behind the Door.

The Boy Comes for His Quarter.

Chapter 8
Strange Goings-On

The next morning just after Sebastian had opened the door for Mr. Usher, the bell rang again. Sebastian flung the door open and saw the boy with the tambourine who had led Heidi to the church tower.

"What do you want?" he asked.

"I came to see Clara," he said. "She owes me a quarter."

Sebastian accused the boy of lying and said he had no idea what the boy could be talking about. But the boy insisted, and Sebastian soon came to the conclusion that this had something to do with Heidi's adventure the day before. So he showed the boy to the study.

Miss Rottenmeier was in another room when she thought she heard the sound of a tambourine coming from the study. She entered the room and could hardly believe her eyes.

"Stop, stop at once!" she cried when she saw the raggedy boy playing his tambourine for Heidi and Clara. She ran towards the boy, but tripped on something on the floor. Looking down, she saw to her horror a strange, dark object at her feet. It was the tortoise. She leaped in the air to avoid it, then she screamed at the top of her lungs for Sebastian. He was just outside the door, doubled up with laughter. When he came into the room, Miss Rottenmeier had collapsed onto a chair.

"Get rid of that boy and his animal at once!" she ordered.

Miss Rottenmeier Trips on the Tortoise.

HEIDI

Sebastian led the boy to the door and put some coins into his hand to thank him for his music.

In the meantime, Clara, Heidi and Mr. Usher continued their lessons, and Miss Rottenmeier stayed in the study to supervise.

In a little while, Sebastian returned and handed Clara a big basket. He explained that someone had dropped it off at the house and it was for her. Clara opened the lid, and suddenly the room was swarming with kittens. The jumped out one after another and rushed madly about, some biting Mr. Usher's pants, and others climbing up Miss Rottenmeier's skirt. The whole room was in an uproar, and Clara was delighted.

At this point Miss Rottenmeier began to shriek. She called for Sebastian and Tinette to get rid of the animals at once. They came and put the kittens back in the basket and hid them in the attic with the other two.

Swarming with Kittens

HEIDI

Then Miss Rottenmeier turned to Heidi.

"Adelheid," she said very sternly, "I can think of only one punishment for such a little savage as you. Perhaps a spell in the dark cellar among the bats and rats will tame you and teach you to behave."

Clara protested loudly. "Please wait till Papa comes home! He will be here very soon, and I'll tell him everything, and he'll decide what is to be done."

Miss Rottenmeier knew that she could not object to what Clara was saying, for Mr. Seseman would be very angry if he heard that Clara had been upset over this matter. So Miss Rottenmeier agreed, but she added that she too would talk with Clara's father when he arrived.

Heidi still could not understand what she had done wrong. But she became very sad and fell asleep dreaming about her home so far away.

Dreams of Her Mountain Home

Mr. Seseman Returns.

Chapter 9
A Bad Report to Mr. Seseman

A few days later Mr. Seseman arrived at the house. The first thing he did when he got inside was to go and find Clara. He hugged his little girl and told her how much he had missed her. Then he turned to Heidi, who was standing beside Clara, and shook her hand.

He asked Heidi if she and Clara got along well. Heidi nodded her head and said that Clara was a good friend. Mr. Seseman smiled and told the girls that he would eat dinner and join them later on.

HEIDI

He went along to the dining room, where Miss Rottenmeier was making sure that everything was in order. When he sat down, the housekeeper lost no time telling him about what had happened in the last few days. She went on to tell him that she thought Heidi was a disgraceful child. But Mr. Seseman knew Miss Rottenmeier quite well and paid little attention to her complaints. Finally, she told him that she did not think that Heidi was right in the head.

Mr. Seseman had not taken her earlier complaints seriously but this was another matter. If it was true, Clara could come to some harm. Since he didn't really trust Miss Rottenmeier's judgment, he decided to talk to Heidi himself.

Mr. Seseman finished his meal quickly and excused himself. He then went into the study to have a talk first with Clara. Since Heidi was there with Clara, he thought for a

Miss Rottenmeier Tells What Has Happened.

moment. It would be difficult to ask Clara about her friend while she was still in the room, so Mr. Seseman asked Heidi to bring him a glass of water.

"Fresh water?" asked Heidi.

"Oh yes—fresh water," he answered.

After Heidi left the room, he pulled his chair closer to his daughter and stroked her hand. Then in a kind voice, he asked Clara to tell him all about the animals, the street musician, and Heidi's strange behavior. Clara explained everything. When she was finished, her father laughed heartily.

"Well, well, then you don't want me to send her home. You're not tired of her?"

"No, no, Papa," she exclaimed, "since Heidi's been here, all sorts of wonderful things have happened. It's really fun having her here. She tells me wonderful stories about her life on the mountain and her grandfather."

Heidi Goes for Water.

HEIDI

Just then, in walked Heidi. She had walked all the way to the village fountain in order to get Mr. Seseman a glass of really fresh water. Heidi told Clara and her father of the kind man she met who asked her who she was and why she was carrying water back to the house. The man had a nice smile, wore a thick gold chain, and carried a walking stick. Clara immediately recognized him as her doctor. Mr. Seseman smiled at the thought of what his old friend would have to say about this unusual search for water to quench his thirst.

That evening he informed Miss Rottenmeier that Heidi was to stay. He said he found her perfectly normal, and he thought she would be a suitable friend for Clara. He also added that she should be treated with kindness at all times. Then he informed everyone that his mother, Clara's grandmother, would be coming to visit after he left on his business trip.

Really Fresh Water!

A Kind Grandmother

Chapter 10
Grandma's Visit

Clara could hardly control her excitement when she learned of her grandmother's visit. She told Heidi all about her and how much fun it would be to have her in the house again.

When the day finally came, even Heidi was excited about Grandma's visit. As soon as Heidi saw the old woman, she loved her at once. She saw the kind expression in her eyes and the way her white hair curled in tiny ringlets about her face. And Grandma liked Heidi too. Despite Miss Rottenmeier's harsh words, Grandma knew that Heidi was a bright and loving child.

Not long after Grandma arrived, she discovered that while Clara took her afternoon nap, Heidi was left with nothing to do. The child still had not learned to read, and this concerned Grandma. She could not understand why this was so. She called Heidi downstairs and asked her to sit next to her while they looked at picture books. Heidi was happy to have company in the afternoon and liked all the lovely pictures Grandma showed her. But then they came to a picture of a green meadow with goats and sheep and a young shepherd, Heidi burst into tears. It reminded her of the home she loved so much, and Peter and Grandfather, who were now so far away.

Grandma dried her tears and decided to ask her why she had not learned to read.

Heidi confessed that she knew she could

Looking at Picture Books

never learn to read, since Peter had told her how hard he tried but could never learn either. Grandma told her that of course she could learn, and that she must try. She asked Heidi if she would like to read the story that went with the picture of the green meadow and the animals. Heidi thought about it for a minute. How wonderful it would be if she could spend her lonely afternoons reading stories about faraway places!

One morning about a week later, Mr. Usher asked if he could speak with Grandma. He was invited to her room, where he was greeted in the usual friendly way.

"I have something quite remarkable to report," he said. "The impossible has happened. Heidi has learned to read at last. I never thought I would see the day!"

Grandma smiled. That evening she gave Heidi the picture book as a present, and Heidi read the story about the meadow to Clara.

Something Remarkable to Report

A Big Library Filled with Books

Chapter 11
The Joy of Reading

As soon as Heidi learned how to read, she found that life in **Mr.** Seseman's big house was not so lonely. Now she had friends to keep her company when she was alone in this strange city.

Downstairs in the study there was a big library filled with many books. Some were too long or too difficult for Heidi to read, but there were many she could enjoy. Every afternoon, Grandma would take Heidi aside and ask her if she had finished her last book. If she had, Grandma would take Heidi's hand, and the two of them would go downstairs to the library and choose a new book.

HEIDI

In the evenings, Heidi would take turns reading with Clara and Grandma. Sometimes they would all read a whole book out loud. It made Clara very proud that her friend finally had learned to read, and now they could share the many wonderful things that books had to offer.

But no matter how many books Heidi read, the one Grandma gave her was always her favorite. She read it over and over and kept it in a special place in her room. When she returned to the mountain, she would read it to Grannie.

Mr. Usher now had an easy time with Clara's lessons. Since Heidi had learned to read, the time went much faster, and Clara and Heidi were both eager to learn and full of questions.

Sometimes Mr. Usher would ask Heidi to read a long and difficult passage loud. He

Reading Aloud

was always pleased when she was able to do it easily.

Although the books helped ease Heidi's loneliness, they could not stop her from thinking about Grandfather and her home in the mountains. Every time she looked at her picture book and saw the green meadows and the sheep, her heart longed to return to where she belonged.

Heidi Longs for the Mountains.

A Sad Day for Heidi and Clara

Chapter 12
The House Is Haunted!

Not long after Heidi learned how to read, Grandma announced that she would be leaving. The day of her departure was a sad time for Heidi and Clara. They knew things would not be the same without Grandma. Soon after the old woman left, Heidi began to get very homesick. Every night she cried herself to sleep thinking about her home on the mountain. Sometimes she woke up shaking at the thought that Uncle Alp or Grannie might be sick, or that they would die before she returned. Things got so bad that she grew pale and thin. Even Sebastian looked worried when he saw her pushing her food away.

At about this time, strange things began to happen inside the house. Every morning Sebastian found the front door unlocked and standing wide open. Nothing inside the house was ever missing, so he was sure it wasn't a thief. Some of the servants began to worry.

One evening when Sebastian was up late, he saw a white figure on the stairs. Soon even Miss Rottenmeier was frightened. She wrote Mr. Seseman and asked him to come home at once. But Mr. Seseman did not take her strange story at all seriously. So Miss Rottenmeier told Clara about the open door and the white figure. Clara became so upset that Miss Rottenmeier wrote to Mr. Seseman saying that she feared for Clara's health. This time he believed her and came home at once.

Sure enough, after Mr. Seseman arrived,

Sebastian Finds the Door Open!

he noticed that the front door was unbolted and standing open every morning. He became concerned about this strange occurrence and decided to get to the bottom of things.

The next evening, Mr. Seseman invited his friend, Clara's doctor, to sit up with him and wait for the ghost. The doctor arrived promptly at eight, and the two men sat up talking and drinking strong coffee. Some time after twelve, they heard the distinct sound of a bolt being unlatched. Mr. Seseman exchanged looks with the doctor, and they walked slowly towards the front door.

"Who's there?" asked Mr. Seseman.

The figure turned and gave a little cry. It was Heidi, barefooted and wearing her white nightgown. She began to tremble when she saw the two men.

"Why, Heidi, what are you doing here?" asked the doctor.

"I—I don't know," stammered Heidi.

"Heidi, What Are You Doing Here?"

HEIDI

The doctor took Heidi by the hand and led her away from the door. He talked in a kind voice for a little while. He soon discovered that Heidi had been sleepwalking. She was the ghost that everyone feared so much! After he finished asking her several questions, the doctor realized that Heidi was very homesick—so homesick that her health was beginning to suffer. The sleepwalking was really a symptom of her unhappiness and her longing to escape and return to Grandfather.

The doctor spoke with Mr. Seseman. He explained that Heidi must be allowed to return to the mountain.

"Just look at the child," he said. "She is pale and has lost several pounds in a short time. Without knowing it she has been opening the front door every night. She should be sent home tomorrow. That's my prescription."

Mr. Seseman looked very upset. He knew how much Heidi meant to Clara, but he also

Heidi Was the Ghost!

knew that what the doctor was saying was true. He simply could not be responsible for Heidi becoming ill. He thought for a short time and then turned to his friend and said:

"I know how upset this will make Clara, but I can see how things are. Heidi will leave for her home in the morning."

The Doctor Warns Mr. Seseman.

Miss Rottenmeier Packs Heidi's Trunk.

Chapter 13
Home Again

Mr. Seseman was true to his word, and the very next morning he made arrangements for Heidi's departure. He had Miss Rottenmeier pack her trunk, and he went upstairs to tell Clara the news.

Clara was very distressed by the news, and she tried to make her father change his mind. But she soon saw that he really was right. He promised Clara that he would take her to visit Heidi the following year. This made Clara feel a little better. Then she asked if she could put some nice things in

HEIDI

Heidi's trunk. Mr. Seseman agreed and left Clara to be alone with her plans for gifts for Heidi and her friends at home.

When Heidi found out about the journey, she became so excited she could hardly eat a thing. She was not sure whether she was really awake or just dreaming. But when Sebastian brought down her trunk, she knew everything was real.

Clara packed some warm blankets, dresses, hankies and sewing things for Heidi. Then she showed her the special surprise. It was a big basket of soft white rolls for Grannie. Heidi kissed Clara warmly and held her hand, and the two friends said their good-byes.

Since the trip back to Dorfli was a long one, Sebastian offered to go with Heidi. They took a train from the city and didn't arrive in Dorfli until the next day. Heidi held the basket with the rolls on her lap the whole time. She worried that Grannie might be sick or even

Clara's Special Surprise

dead. But as the train chugged to a stop, she became excited and happy.

When they reached the station, Sebastian asked an old man driving a carriage which was the best way to get to Dorfli. The old man said he would take them there. Sebastian wasn't completely sure that the roads were safe in this country town. But Heidi knew that the roads were passable this time of year and offered to continue the journey on her own. Sebastian loaded her trunk onto the carriage and handed her a fat packet and a letter for her grandfather.

"The packet is for you. It's a present from Mr. Seseman. The letter is for your grandfather. It will explain everything," said Sebastian as he bent down to kiss Heidi good-bye.

The man with the carriage was the baker from Dorfli. He had known Heidi's parents

The Train Arrives in Dorfli.

HEIDI

and realized at once who she was. They chatted a little bit as the horse pulled them up the hill to the village. When they reached Dorfli, the baker lifted Heidi down. She thanked him and told him that Grandfather would pick up the trunk later.

As soon as the carriage pulled away, Heidi rushed uphill as fast as she could go. She had to stop every now and then to catch her breath, for her basket was heavy and the mountain was very steep. But all she could think about was Grannie.

When she reached the hut, she raced up to the door but could hardly open it because she was trembling so much. But she managed it and threw into the little room quite out of breath and unable to say a word.

"Goodness me," someone said from a corner of the room, "that was how Heidi used to come in. How I miss her!"

"It's me—Heidi!" she cried and threw

Heidi Rushes to Grannie.

herself on the old woman's lap and hugged her. She was so happy she could hardly speak. Grannie was so surprised she could not speak either. She stroked Heidi's hair, and a few big tears from her old blind eyes fell onto Heidi's hand.

"It's really you, child," she said.

"Yes, really and truly, Grannie. Don't cry. I'm here and I'll never go away again," said Heidi as she held back her own tears.

Then Heidi handed Grannie the basket and brought out the rolls. One by one she laid them on Grannie's lap.

"Now you won't have to eat hard bread for a while," she said.

Grannie smiled. She could hardly believe all this was really happening. Just then Peter's mother came into the hut. She rushed to Heidi and gave her a big kiss. Heidi talked with the two women for a little while, then said good-bye and began the long climb up

"It's Really You, Heidi!"

the mountain to Grandfather.

The air was cool as Heidi made her way up the steep hill. Everything seemed even more beautiful than she remembered. The peaks of the mountains were snow-covered, the pasture land and the valley below were all red and gold, and there were pink clouds floating in the sky. It was all so lovely that Heidi stood with tears pouring down her cheeks as she breathed in the fragrant air.

Soon, she could see the tops of the fir trees, then the roof, then the whole hut, and then Grandfather himself. He was sitting on the bench outside and smoking his pipe, just as he used to do. Heidi ran towards him and flung her arms around him. For the first time in years his eyes were wet with tears of gladness. He sat Heidi on his knee and looked her over.

"So you've come back, Heidi," he said, "and you don't look so very grand either. Did they

Home Again!

HEIDI

send you away?"

Heidi told Grandfather everything about her life with Clara and how kind they all were to her. Then she told him about her homesickness and the doctor's advice. When she finished, she ran and brought him Mr. Seseman's letter and the packet.

Uncle Alp read the letter and put it in his pocket without saying a word. He told Heidi that the packet contained money for her to use as she wished. Then Heidi and her grandfather sat down and had a big mug of milk and some bread with melted cheese. It was the first time Heidi had had an appetite in a long time.

After a little while, Heidi heard a shrill whistle. She ran out and saw Peter coming down the path surrounded by his lively goats. When he saw her, he stopped dead and stared in astonishment.

As soon as he could get his voice back,

Uncle Alp Reads the Letter.

HEIDI

Peter told Heidi how happy he was to see her again, and the two friends chatted for a while as they watched the sun go down.

When she went inside again, Heidi found that her grandfather had made her a lovely sweet-smelling bed and had covered it with clean linen sheets When she lay down to sleep it was as if she had never been away at all.

Peter Is Happy Heidi Is Home.

Out in the Wonderful Alpine Air

Chapter 14
An Important Day for Grandfather

Heidi stood under the swaying trees, waiting for her grandfather to go down the mountain with her. He was going to fetch her trunk from Dorfli while she visited Grannie. The day was crisp and clear, and Heidi tried to take it all in—the mountains, the fir trees, and the wonderful alpine air.

Soon Grandfather was ready, and they walked down the mountain together. Grannie was overjoyed to see Heidi again, and she told her how much she had enjoyed the soft white rolls from the city. Heidi only wished that she had enough rolls so that Grannie would never have to eat hard bread again. Then she remembered the money that Mr. Seseman had given her. A beaming smile spread over Heidi's face. She would give the money to Peter so that every day he could bring Grannie a fresh white roll from the village. Of course, Grannie protested when she heard this idea. She didn't want Heidi to spend her money on rolls, but when she saw how excited the child was, she agreed.

To entertain the old woman, Heidi reached up on a shelf and brought down a book of hymns. Now that she had learned to read, she could read Grannie her favorite hymns. This made the old woman so happy that she could hardly speak. So for the rest of the day, Heidi chatted with Grannie and read her hymns from the old book.

Soon Grandfather came and tapped on the window to tell Heidi it was time to go home.

Heidi Reads Hymns to Grannie.

HEIDI

On the way back up the mountain, Heidi had so much to tell her grandfather that she talked until they reached the hut. She told Grandfather about her idea for using the money Mr. Seseman had given her. Grandfather smiled when he saw how generous and kind-hearted Heidi was.

That evening at dinner, as Heidi chatted about her life in the city and how kind everyone had been to her, a change came over Grandfather. For the first time in a very long while, he saw the goodness in other people. And he saw this goodness through Heidi's eyes. He realized what a gift this child was, and that his life of bitterness was not good for him and certainly not good for Heidi.

That night Uncle Alp made an important decision. He decided to return to a life that included other people.

The next day was Sunday, and Grandfather told Heidi to get dressed in the clothes Clara

Uncle Alp Makes a Decision.

had given her. Then he took his old blue suit out of the closet. He shined the old brass buttons and even put on a hat. Then together, Grandfather and Heidi walked down the mountain and into the church in the village.

The people of Dorfli were already in church, and the singing had started as Heidi and Uncle Alp went in and sat down in the back. The hymn was hardly over before people were nudging one another and whispering that Uncle Alp was in church. Everyone kept turning around to stare at the old man with the little girl.

When the service was over, Grandfather took Heidi's hand and they went to see the pastor together. They were welcomed into the house by the kind man, and Grandfather first apologized for his behavior so many months ago, when the pastor had come to ask him to send Heidi to school. After a long talk, the two men shook hands, and Uncle Alp agreed

All Dressed Up

to move down to the village during the win
ter so that Heidi could attend school. A
Uncle Alp stood in the doorway shaking the
pastor's hand, the people of the village
crowded around and offered their best wishes
to the old man and Heidi. They could see tha
something had changed Uncle Alp, and when
they heard that he planned to return to Dor
fli to live among them, they all wished him
well and offered to help with the move.

When at last he and Heidi started fo
home, many people went part of the way with
them, and when they said good-bye, they
asked him to visit them in their homes before
long. As he watched them go, Heidi saw such
a kind light in his eye that she said:

"Grandfather, you look so different—so
peaceful. I've never seen you look this way
before."

Grandfather smiled and explained that he
was happier today than he had been in a very

The Villagers Welcome Uncle Alp.

long time. He had finally given up the bitterness that had made him a lonely old man without friends or neighbors. Now, thanks to Heidi, that was all over. He had begun a new life.

When they reached Peter's cottage, Grandfather went in.

"Good day, Grannie," he said. "I can see I must get busy with some more repairs before the autumn winds begin to blow.

"Goodness me, is it Uncle Alp?" cried the old woman. "What a fine surprise! Now I can thank you in person for all you've done for us."

She held out her hand, which trembled a little, and he shook it heartily. At last the two people Heidi loved most were friends.

Making Friends

The Doctor Is Sad.

Chapter 15
Preparation for a Journey

One sunny September morning, the kind doctor who had been responsible for Heidi being sent home walked along the street to the Seseman's house. It was the sort of day on which everyone should have been happy. But the doctor hung his head in sadness. His hair had grown whiter since the spring, and he wore an air of great sadness. His only daughter had died recently. She had been the great joy of his life since his wife had died some time before. Now he just could not seem to be able to recover his spirits.

HEIDI

Sebastian opened the door and showed him in. Mr. Seseman greeted him in the hall. The two old friends shook hands, and Mr. Seseman could see how unhappy the doctor was.

"I'm glad to see you, doctor. I want to talk to you about the trip to the mountains. Haven't you changed your mind now that Clara seems so much better?"

The doctor became impatient, but he was careful not to lose his temper as he explained to his friend that the long journey to visit Heidi would be more than Clara could take.

Mr. Seseman knew the doctor was right. But he also knew how much this trip meant to his daughter. He just did not have the heart to tell her she would not be able to go.

Then Mr. Seseman had an idea. Why not send the doctor in Clara's place? His friend was looking so poorly that the fresh mountain air and a change of scene would do him a world of good. Besides, he could visit Heidi

The Journey Would Be Too Much for Clara.

and bring back all the news to Clara. When he suggested this to his friend, the doctor thought for a moment, then agreed. Mr. Seseman was pleased with this new plan and hoped Clara would not be too sad.

When she learned that she could not make the trip herself, Clara could not keep the tears from her eyes. But she was told that the trip would only make her health worse, so she blinked back the tears and turned to the doctor.

"Oh please go see Heidi for me. When you come back, you'll be able to tell me all about your trip, and it will be almost as if I'd been there myself."

Then Clara began planning what little presents she would give the doctor to take to Heidi and her friends.

The packing was no easy task, for there were many things that Clara wanted to include. First there was a thick coat with a

Mr. Seseman Tells Clara.

hood, so that Heidi could go and visit Grannie during the winter. Next came a warm shawl for Grannie to wrap herself in when the cold winds howled around the small cottage. Then there was the box of little cakes for her to eat with her coffee and an enormous sausage for Peter's mother to share with Grannie and Peter. There was a pouch of tobacco for Grandfather and a lot of little surprise packets for Heidi.

The packing was soon done, and Clara waited anxiously for the doctor to pick up the trunk and depart for the mountains.

Presents for Heidi

Heidi Runs to the Doctor.

Chapter 16
A Visitor for Heidi

The cool, crisp mountain air brushed against the doctor's cheeks as he made his way up the mountain to Uncle Alp's hut. He had written Heidi that he would be coming, and she was eagerly awaiting him. As he saw the fir trees swaying at the top of the mountain, he thought he saw someone running towards him. Sure enough, in a few minutes he could see Heidi running down the mountain, waving her hands and shouting to him.

As soon as she was close enough, Heidi jumped up and gave the doctor a warm hug.

HEIDI

He had not expected such a reception, and he thanked her for welcoming him to her home. Heidi was full of questions about Clara, Mr. Seseman, Grandma and even Miss Rottenmeier. The doctor could hardly answer her, since she was so excited she didn't give him a chance to catch his breath.

They went towards the hut hand in hand. But even in her excitement, Heidi could sense the sadness in the doctor's eyes. She knew that something must be making him unhappy, and she made up her mind that during his stay she would make him smile again.

When she introduced Grandfather to the doctor, the two men exchanged handshakes and became friends at once. Heidi had told each one so much about the other that they hardly felt like strangers at all.

Then the doctor gave Heidi the presents Clara had sent her. She loved the winter coat and was looking forward to bringing Grannie

Walking to the Hut

the warm shawl the very next day.

The next morning the doctor climbed up to the goat pastures with Heidi. She chatted away all the time about the goats and their strange little ways and the mountain peaks and the flowers. Heidi led the way to her favorite spot, from which she could look down on the distant valley and up to the great mountains where the snow sparkled in the sunlight.

She sat down beside the doctor and asked him if he thought the home as beautiful as she herself did.

"Yes, Heidi, it's very beautiful here," he agreed, "but can a heart forget its sorrow and be happy even here?"

"No one is sad here, not when there is so much beauty and so much love. Stay with us for a little while and you will see," she said.

The doctor was touched by Heidi's words. He surely had nothing to lose. Life in the city

Heidi's Favorite Place

had become unbearable for him since his daughter's death. He decided to give himself a rest here in the mountains and to enjoy Uncle Alp's hospitality.

The weather was fine and sunny all month, and the doctor went up to the hut every morning and from there went off on long walks with Uncle Alp. Together they climbed high where the fir trees were storm-tossed, and higher still to where the hawks nested. Uncle Alp told the doctor many things about the mountains and about his own life. Soon the two men shared a special friendship. The healthy air, good food, and friendly company began to work like Heidi said they would. The twinkle came back into the doctor's eyes, and his cheeks glowed with a healthy pink color.

With the last day of September, the holiday came to an end. On the day before his return to the city, the doctor appeared at the hut

Climbing to Where the Hawks Nest

looking very sad. He was sorry to go, for he had felt at home on the mountain. Uncle Alp was going to miss him too, and Heidi had grown so accustomed to seeing him every day that she could hardly believe those pleasant times were over. But the doctor promised both his friends that he would return very soon.

He thanked them both for making his vacation so wonderful and went on his way. Heidi stood beneath a fir tree and waved until all she could see was a speck in the distance. As he turned for the last time to wave back, the doctor thought to himself:

"This is certainly a wonderful place for sick minds as well as bodies. Life really seems worth living again!"

Waving Good-Bye

Snow to the Windowsills

Chapter 17
Winter in Dorfli

The snow lay so deep on the mountain
that winter that Peter's hut was buried in
it up to the windowsills. Fresh snow fell
almost every night, so on most mornings
he had to jump out of the living room window to leave the house. Uncle Alp remembered his promise to the pastor, and as
soon as the first snow fell, he took Heidi
and the goats down to the village for the
rest of the winter.

Near the church in Dorfli, there was a
large, rambling, ramshackle place, almost in
ruins. Uncle Alp saw the house and knew

that with some repairs and hard work it would be a fine home. So he rented it and began to make it livable. He put up some wooden partitions and laid straw on the floor to make winter quarters for the goats in the back of the house. Inside, he repaired the great oak door and patched up the walls and floors. Heidi loved the house, which was much bigger than the small hut on the mountain. She invited Peter over to explore the place with her. Together, they discovered every little nook and cranny until there were no surprises in the new house.

There was much to do in the winter house, and Heidi was starting school. She soon got used to living in the village and going to classes every day. Peter, on the other hand, was hardly ever in school. Heidi noticed his absences, and she also knew that he still had not learned how to read. So one evening when she was visiting Grannie, she took

Uncle Alp Makes the House Livable.

Peter aside.

"I've thought of something," she said.

"What?" Peter asked.

"You must learn to read."

"I have learned," Peter answered.

"I mean properly, so that you can read anything," she insisted.

"Can't be done," Peter said.

"I don't believe that any more," she told him squarely, "and neither does anyone else. Clara's grandma told me it wasn't so and she was right."

Peter looked surprised at Heidi's tone. She seemed so sure of herself. Then she offered to help him learn to read, so that he could surprise Grannie, who was feeling ill. At first Peter was stubborn and refused, but when he saw how much it meant to Heidi and how good it would be for Grannie, he agreed.

At once, Heidi was all smiles. She pulled him over to the table, where a book was all

Heidi Decides to Teach Peter.

ready. It was a rhyming ABC which had come in a big parcel from Clara. Heidi liked it so much that she thought it would be just the thing to teach Peter with. They sat down side by side, bent their heads over the book, and the lesson began. Heidi made Peter go over everything again and again to make sure he knew it all before they went ahead. She knew how difficult it was for him and gave him encouragement every step of the way.

During that winter, Peter came regularly for his lessons and made good progress. The snow became so heavy that Heidi could not go to visit Grannie anymore. She knew the old woman would miss her reading aloud. During this time, Heidi worked extra hard with Peter, who came to the house despite the heavy snows.

One evening he came up from the village and announced to his mother:

Lessons

HEIDI

"I can do it!"

"Do what, Peter?" she asked.

Instead of answering his mother's question, Peter reached up and took Grannie's hymn book off the shelf. In a clear voice, Peter read Grannie her favorite hymn. The two women were speechless. They thought they would never live to see the day that Peter would really learn to read.

The next day Peter went to school, and when the teacher called on him, he read just as well as he had the night before. The teacher was pleased and surprised. He soon learned that Heidi had worked a near miracle with her pupil.

As soon as school was over, the teacher went across to the pastor to tell him the news, and they talked about the good influence that Heidi and her grandfather were having in the village.

Peter Reads Out Loud.

May in the Alps

Chapter 18
More Visitors

The winter passed, and it was May again. The last snows had disappeared, and the little mountain streams raced in full flood down to the valley. The mountainsides were green again and bathed in warm, clear sunlight. The flowers were opening their petals among the fresh green grass.

Heidi was back on the mountain. She listened to the sound of the wind blowing down from the heights, gathering strength as it came nearer. She listened to the hum and buzz of the insects, and everything seemed to

HEIDI

be saying, "It's spring, and we're back on the mountain!"

Soon Heidi's quiet pleasure was interrupted by the bleating of Peter's goats. She ran to meet him and he handed her a letter. The postman had given it to him that morning, and he had almost forgotten to come up the mountain and present it to Heidi.

Heidi looked at the letter carefully, then ran to Grandfather. It was a letter from Clara, which she wanted him to read aloud so they could both share it.

Clara wrote that she would be there in a very short time. Her health had improved, and the doctor had told her it would be safe to travel. She would be coming with Grandma. Heidi was so excited she could hardly speak. She was so overjoyed that she felt she must go down to tell Grannie the wonderful news. It was delightful to go running down the mountainside in the bright sunshine

Sharing the Letter

with the wind at her back.

Grannie was in her usual corner, spinning, but she looked sad and worried. Peter had already told her the news, and she was afraid that Clara was coming to take Heidi back to the city with her. Although the old woman would not admit what was really on her mind, Heidi knew her well enough to realize that something was wrong. So Heidi read to Grannie for a long time, and when the old woman saw how happy the child was, the troubled look left her face.

It was dusk when Heidi went home, and the stars came out one by one as she climbed up to the hut. She stopped to gaze up at them, feeling a deep peacefulness inside. She was thankful to be alive and to be here in the place she loved so much.

Gazing at the Stars

A Remarkable Procession

Chapter 19
Clara Arrives

May passed, and June came with longer days and hotter sun, which brought the flowers out all over the mountain. They filled the air with their sweet scents. Heidi came out of the hut looking for some flowers to place on the table when she gave a shout which brought Grandfather running.

"Come and look! Come and look!" she shouted.

When he looked in the direction she was pointing, he saw a remarkable procession coming up the mountain. First came two men, carrying between them a chair on poles, and in it sat a girl, very-carefully wrapped up. A stately-looking woman rode on horseback behind them, gazing about with interest. Then came two more men, one pushing an empty wheelchair and the other carrying an enormous bundle of rugs and wraps in a basket on his back.

Heidi knew at once that Clara had finally arrived. She ran across the grass to welcome her friend. When Heidi reached Clara, the two girls hugged each other and shouted for joy. Heidi turned to Grandma Seseman and gave the old woman a welcoming embrace.

"My dear Uncle Alp," Grandma exclaimed, "what a magnificent place to live! I can't imagine anything more beautiful. And Heidi looks so wonderful. It does me good to see her here where she belongs."

Uncle Alp smiled and welcomed Clara and her grandmother. Then he brought the

Heidi and Clara Hug Each Other.

wheelchair forward and spread some rugs in it. He asked Clara if he could carry her the rest of the way in her usual chair. She consented and they all made their way up to the hut.

Clara could not take her eyes off the scene which stretched before her. She had spent all of her life cooped up inside a house in the city. All this beauty was quite new and remarkable to her.

"Oh, Heidi, if only I could run about with you and look at all the things I know so well from what you have told me!" Clara said.

Heidi took hold of Clara's chair, and pushing with all her might, she managed to get it as far as the fir trees. Both Clara and Grandma stopped and admired the tall, majestic trees. Then Heidi wheeled Clara over to the goat-stall and opened the door wide so that she could have a good look inside.

Under the Fir Trees

HEIDI

Clara could not seem to get enough of all the sights Heidi showed her. She asked her grandmother if she could only stay on a little longer so that she could see the meadows and meet Peter and Grannie. But Grandma Seseman just smiled and told Clara to enjoy what she could and not to think about anything else.

During the tour of inspection, Grandfather had arranged the table and chair and put everything out for their meal. Milk and cheese were warming on the stove, and before long everyone sat down to dinner. Grandma was delighted with the unusual "dining room" with its view of the valley and mountain peaks. Clara ate heartily and exclaimed that nothing in the city had ever tasted so good.

"Just keep it up," said Grandfather. "It's our good mountain air—it more than makes up for our cooking!"

A Hearty Dinner

HEIDI

Grandma and Uncle Alp chatted while the two girls exchanged news of their own. Soon Grandma looked towards the west and said:

"We shall have to go very soon, Clara. The sun is going-down, and the men will be back any moment with the horse and your chair."

Clara's face fell when she realized that she would have to leave so soon. There were still so many things she hadn't seen, and she wanted to spend much more time with Heidi.

Uncle Alp glanced at Clara, then he turned to her grandmother.

"I've been thinking," he began, "and I hope you won't object to the suggestion. Suppose you leave Clara here for a while. I'm sure the mountain air will do her good. You brought so many rugs and blankets with you that we could easily make her a comfortable bed. And I promise to look after her and give her all the attention she needs."

Clara and Heidi were overjoyed at his

Clara Doesn't Want to Leave.

words, and Grandma was beaming as she nodded her head in consent. She knew that being here with Heidi and Uncle Alp would be good medicine for her sickly grand-daugter.

Heidi and Clara at once began making plans, and Uncle Alp and Grandma prepared a bed for Clara next to Heidi's up in the loft.

The loveliest moment of the day came after everyone bid farewell to Grandma. Clara was in the hayloft, looking straight out to the starry sky.

"Oh, Heidi," she said, "it feels as if we were riding in a carriage right to heaven."

Clara lay awake long after Heidi was fast asleep. She looked up at the black sky and watched the stars until she finally fell into a deep, restful sleep.

Clara Looks at the Sky.

Steaming Mugs of Milk for Breakfast

Chapter 20
Clara Begins to Enjoy Life

As the sun rose the next morning, Uncle Alp was outside as usual, quietly watching the mists drift over the mountains and the light clouds grow pink as day broke. Then he went inside to see how his guest was doing.

Clara had just opened her eyes and was gazing with astonishment at the sunbeams dancing on the bed. Uncle Alp asked her if she had had a good night's sleep.

"Oh yes," she replied. "I didn't wake up once during the night."

For breakfast, Uncle Alp served the girls

steaming mugs of milk. At first Clara was a little reluctant to drink goat's milk, since she had never tasted it before, but when she saw Heidi drink with such pleasure, she tried it too. The milk was delicious. It tasted as sweet and spicy as if it had sugar and cinnamon in it.

Clara and Heidi had so many plans that they did not know where to begin. But Heidi thought they should first write to Grandma as they had promised to do every day. So the two girls sat outside in the warm sunshine and wrote letters. Clara's eyes kept straying. It was all so wonderful. The wind had died down, and only a gentle breeze fanned her cheeks and whispered through the trees.

The morning passed in a flash, and Uncle Alp brought them two bowls of milk, saying that Clara should stay out of doors as long as it was light. So they had another hearty meal outside. Afterward, Heidi wheeled

Writing to Grandma

HEIDI

Clara under the shade of the fir trees, where they spent the afternoon telling each other everything that had happened since Heidi left the city.

And so, Heidi and Clara passed two weeks, sitting outside, talking, eating big meals, and enjoying life on the mountain. After a while, Uncle Alp noticed a distinct improvement in Clara's health. She began to look more robust, and she had a rosy glow to her cheeks. So the old man began trying to get Clara on her feet every morning before putting her in her chair. At first, Clara was afraid to stand alone, since it hurt her, but each day she tried a little harder.

Soon Uncle Alp promised the two girls that he would take them up to the pastures.

Uncle Alp Helps Clara to Her Feet.

Uncle Alp Brings Out Clara's Wheelchair.

Chapter 21
The Unexpected Happens

Uncle Alp stood outside the next morning. He looked up at the sky to make sure it would be good weather for the journey up the mountain to the pastures. The girls were looking forward to the trip so much that he hated to disappoint them. But it looked like a fine day, so he brought out Clara's wheelchair and put it in front of the hut before going inside to wake the girls.

After a big breakfast, Heidi, Clara and Grandfather began the trip up the mountain. When they reached the pasture, they saw the goats grazing peacefully in little groups and Peter stretched out full length on the ground.

"Now enjoy yourselves," said Uncle Alp, as he prepared to leave them. "Your dinner is in the bag over there in the shade."

There was not a cloud in the deep blue sky. The two girls sat side by side, as happy and contented as could be. From time to time one of the goats came and lay down beside them. After a while, Heidi asked Clara if she would mind waiting while she ran up to the meadow to pick flowers. Clara told Heidi it was fine, and that she would enjoy sitting peacefully and feeding the goats. To Clara, this strange new experience was very exciting. To be here, all by herself, and out of doors in such a beautiful place, with a little goat eating so trustfully out of her hand, was all so delightful. She had never expected to know such happiness and it gave her a new

Sitting and Feeding the Goats

idea of what it must mean to be like other girls, healthy and free. The thought seemed to add something special to the day and to her own happiness.

Suddenly Heidi raced back to Clara.

"Oh, the flowers are so beautiful, you simply must come and see them too. Do you think I can carry you?"

Clara shook her head. She knew that Heidi was too small to carry her, and the chair could never be wheeled up the steep incline. She wanted to walk more than ever now!

Heidi called up to Peter, who came down to the pasture. She told him to hold Clara up on one side, while she took the other. Together they helped her to her feet. So far, so good, but Clara could not keep upright without support.

They tried several different methods, but still, Clara flopped heavily between them. Since Peter was taller than Heidi, Clara was

Peter and Heidi Hold Clara Up.

up on one side and down on the other. She tried putting one foot in front of the other, but she drew it back quickly.

"Try just putting one foot down firmly," said Heidi. "I'm sure it would hurt less."

Clara took Heidi's advice, and sure enough, it really did not hurt half so much.

"Try again," urged Heidi, and Clara did so, taking several more steps.

"Oh, Heidi," she cried, "look at me. I'm walking!"

"Yes you are, you are! All by yourself! Oh, I wish Grandfather was here!"

Clara still kept hold of Heidi and Peter, but with each step they could feel her getting steadier on her feet. Heidi was quite wild with excitement.

"Now we can come up to the pasture every day and wander about wherever we like," Heidi exclaimed, "and you'll never have to be pushed about in a wheelchair again. Oh, isn't

"I Can Walk!"

it wonderful?"

And Clara agreed from the bottom of her heart. Nothing could have been more wonderful to her than to be strong and able to move around like other people.

It was not much farther to Heidi's special spot, where Clara was able to sit down on the warm grass among all the beautiful flowers. She was so affected by all that had happened to her that she was silent as she gazed at all the lovely colors and smelled the delicious scents.

After a while, Clara, Heidi and Peter unpacked the lunch Grandfather had given them. They were all hungry, but Clara and Heidi were really too excited to eat very much.

Not long after they finished their meal, Uncle Alp arrived to take them home. Heidi saw him coming and ran to meet him, eager to be the first one to tell him the amazing

Too Excited to Eat

news. She was so excited that she could hardly get the words out. But he gathered what she meant at once, and his face lit up. He went over to where Clara was sitting and gave her an understanding smile as he said:

"Something attempted, something won. This proves you are a strong girl. I am very proud."

He gave her some support, and she was able to walk even better than before, but after a short while, he suggested they rest and not overdo on the first day.

That evening, Uncle Alp suggested that the girls write Clara's grandmother. He told them to invite her for a big surprise.

The next days were the happiest Clara had ever known. Her waking thought each morning was, "I am well! I can walk!" Each day she went a little farther alone, and the exercise gave her such an appetite that Uncle Alp gave her seconds at each meal. This pleased

The Happiest Days of Clara's Life

HEIDI

Uncle Alp, and he took a special pride in Clara's recovery. He felt that the mountain air and all the love he and Heidi felt for the girl had helped her get well.

During that week, Heidi visited Grannie to tell her the good news. As happy as the old woman was for Clara, she herself was not feeling well, and it was hard for her to share in the excitement. Her bed was hard and uncomfortable, but she had to stay there all day. She was too ill to work at her spinning wheel. This made Heidi very unhappy, for she could not help thinking about the wonderful bed she had had at Clara's house in the city. It had many fine, fluffy pillows and a soft mattress. Oh, how she wished she could have that very bed for Grannie!

Grannie Does Not Feel Well.

Heidi Cleans Out the Hut.

Chapter 22
Good-Bye for the Present!

Grandma Seseman received the letter from Clara and Heidi and wondered what the big surprise could possibly be. She wrote back that same day and told them she would be leaving the next morning. Peter brought the letter up in the morning. The girls were already up, waiting for him. As soon as they read the news, they began at once to get everything ready for the big day. Heidi spent the morning cleaning out the hut, while Clara sat and watched her. Then the girls got dressed and sat down outside to wait. Uncle

Alp had been out gathering flowers, and he brought back a big bunch to put inside the hut. Heidi kept getting up to see if there was any sign of their visitor, and at last the little procession came into sight. In front was a guide, leading Grandma's horse, and a man with a laden basket walked behind him. When they reached the little plateau on which the hut stood and the old woman saw the children, she cried out with concern:

"Why Clara, where is your chair? What is this all about?"

But as she came towards them, astonishment took the place of anxiety, and she exclaimed:

"You look so wonderful, my dear. I hardly recognize you."

Then Heidi got up—and so did Clara. Both girls walked slowly towards her. Clara walked with only her hand on Heidi's shoulder for support. Grandma looked on in

The Girls Walk to Grandma.

amazement. They turned and walked towards her, and she saw their two rosy faces were glowing with happiness. Half laughing, half crying, Grandma embraced Clara, then Heidi. She could find no words to express her feelings. Then she saw Uncle Alp, who had come outside and was watching with a pleased smile. She took Clara's arm in hers, and together they went to the old man. Grandma was greatly moved at having her granddaughter walk beside her at last. She grasped Uncle Alp's hand and said:

"My dear Uncle, how can we ever thank you! It is your care and nursing that have done this."

"And love and sun and nature," he added.

"And don't forget the lovely goat's milk," put in Clara.

"Your rosy cheeks tell me that," answered her grandmother. "I really find this all so hard to believe. I can't take my eyes off you.

Grandma Cannot Thank Uncle Alp Enough.

It's a miracle. I must telegraph at once to your father and tell him to come here immediately. I won't tell him why. This will be the greatest surprise of his life."

The little party sat down to dinner in front of the hut, and Grandma was told the whole story right from the beginning.

"I still can't believe it!" she kept saying. "This is all just too good to be true."

As it happened, Mr. Seseman also had been planning a surprise. He had finished his business earlier than he expected and missed Clara so much that he had jumped on a train to Dorfli.

After he reached the little village, he set out on foot to Uncle Alp's hut. He was not used to much exercise, and the long climb up the hill was quite exhausting for him. After a long while, he had not even come to Grannie's hut, so he began to think he must have taken the wrong path. He looked about

A Long Climb

anxiously for someone to ask, but there was not a soul in sight, nor a sound to be heard except the humming of insects and the occasional twittering of a bird.

Mr. Seseman grew very hot, and as he stopped to fan himself, Peter came running down the path, but he was in too much of a hurry even to stop and notice the weary traveler. So Mr. Seseman trudged on. He soon reached Grannie's cottage, so he knew that he was on the right path. He went on from there with more energy, and it was not long before he saw the hut with the three fir trees a little way above him. The sight spurred him on, and he stepped out briskly, chuckling to himself at the surprise he hoped to give everyone up at the hut.

As he stepped thankfully toward the level ground on which the hut stood, he saw two people coming towards him, a tall fair girl, leaning on a smaller girl.

Too Busy Running

HEIDI

He stood still and stared. Suddenly his eyes filled with tears. He was strangely reminded of Clara's mother, who had had just such fair hair and delicate white cheeks. He hardly knew whether he was awake or whether he was dreaming.

"Don't you know me, Papa?" Clara asked. "Am I so different? Am I changed?"

At that, he strode towards her and took her in his arms.

"Changed, indeed!" he cried. "Is it possible? Can I believe my eyes?"

He stepped back a few feet to see her better, then drew her close again. His mother joined them, anxious not to miss a single second of this great moment.

"Well, what do you think of that, my son?" she asked, and then she added, "You thought you'd give us a surprise, a lovely one, but as it turns out, it is nothing to the one we were preparing for you, is it now?" She kissed him

"Can I Believe My Eyes?"

warmly as she spoke.

"Now come and meet Uncle Alp. We owe him so much. I believe both he and Heidi were responsible for all this."

Then Mr. Seseman looked down and gave her a big kiss and a hug.

"I am so glad to see you looking well again too. Why, you look as happy and healthy as you did when you first came to stay with us in the city."

Heidi smiled up at him. She was so pleased that it should be here on the mountain that her good friend had found such happiness.

Then Mr. Seseman and Uncle Alp sat down on the small bench outside the hut. The two men had much to talk about. After Mr. Seseman thanked Uncle Alp again and again, he asked him to tell the whole story of Clara's remarkable recovery. He put out his hand and grasped Uncle Alp's large rough one warmly.

"Dear friend," he said, "I am sure that you

Mr. Seseman and Uncle Alp

will understand what I mean when I say that for years I have never known real happiness. What were all my money and my success worth, if they could not make my poor little girl well? Money can only buy things, but it can never bring health or true happiness. Now you and Heidi have given us both something to live for. That can never be repaid. But you must tell me if there is any way I can show my thanks. I will do anything that is in my power to show my gratitude."

Uncle Alp listened quietly, then he replied:

"I have a share, too, in your joy at Clara's recovery. In that lies my reward. There is only one thing I really wish. I am old, and I cannot expect to live much longer. I shall have nothing to leave Heidi when I die. She has no one but me. If you would promise me that Heidi need never have to go and earn her living among strangers—that would be reward enough for me."

Uncle Alp Has Only One Wish.

HEIDI

"That is something you need not even ask," Mr. Seseman answered. "Heidi is already like one of my family. We shall never allow her to be left with strangers. I promise you that. I will make provisions for her during my life and afterwards as well."

"Amen to that," added Grandma, who had stood beside her son during this last part of the conversation.

Then she put her arm around Heidi and asked:

"Have you a wish to be granted?"

"Yes, I have," Heidi replied.

"I am glad. Tell me what it is," answered Grandma.

"The bed I had in the city, with its three pillows and the warm quilt. I would like to have it for Grannie. It would make her so much more comfortable."

"Of course," answered Grandma. "I will telegraph to the city at once and have it sent

Grandma Agrees to Heidi's Wish.

to Grannie's hut in a day or two."

Heidi was so delighted she wanted to run and tell Grannie the good news at once. But Uncle Alp suggested that they all go down and visit the old woman, whom they had really neglected during all the excitement.

Peter saw everyone coming as he looked out the window.

"Oh, dear," sighed Grannie when he told her what he saw, "are they taking Heidi with them back to the city?"

Just then Heidi burst into the hut.

"Grannie, Grannie,'? she cried, "what do you think? My bed from the city is going to be brought here for you."

She expected to see Grannie's face light up at this news, but instead she saw only a sad little smile.

"Oh Heidi, I think I shall die without you," burst out Grannie.

"What's this?" interrupted Grandma Sese-

Peter Sees Everyone Coming.

man. "Heidi is going to stay here with you and Uncle Alp. We shall want to see her too, but we shall come here to visit."

At that, Grannie's face lit up, and she pressed the woman's hand. Heidi hugged her again .

"I did not know there were such good people in the world. It renews my faith in humankind," said Grannie.

Then everyone stood in the hut and shared a very special moment of happiness, love and friendship that none of them would ever forget.

A Special Moment of Happiness

ANNE OF GREEN GABLES

L.M. Montgomery

Contents

About The Author

Lucy Maud Montgomery was born on November 30, 1874 in Clifton (now New London) on Prince Edward Island, a province of Canada. Her mother died when she was a baby, and she was raised by her grandparents.

Young Lucy began writing short stories and verse as a child. Her first poem was published in the local paper when she was fifteen. In her late teens she qualified for a teacher's license at Prince of Wales College in Charlottetown and studied at Dalhousie University in Halifax, Nova Scotia. For three years she worked there as a journalist and teacher.

In 1898 the young career woman returned home to care for her grandmother who was ill. In her spare time she wrote short stories and poems for children's magazines.

Then one day Lucy was leafing through her notebook of plots for a short serial she had been asked to write for a Sunday School paper. A faded entry written years earlier caught her eye: "Elderly couple apply to orphanage for a boy. By mistake a girl is sent them." The result was her touching first novel, *Anne of Green Gables*. Six sequels which detail the marriage and career of the author's lovable heroine followed. They include *Anne of Avonlea, Chronicles of Avonlea, Anne's House of Dreams, Anne of the Island*, and *Anne of Windy Poplars*.

In 1911 the author married a minister, Reverend Ewan MacDonald, and moved to Toronto, Canada. However, she never stopped missing picturesque Prince Edward Island which is the scene of all but one of her twenty-one novels.

Anne of Green Gables, considered Lucy Montgomery's masterpiece, won her international acclaim. The book has been filmed, translated into five languages, and transcribed into Braille.

The recipient of numerous prestigious awards, the author died at 67 on April 24, 1942.

And Notice She Did!

Chapter One

The News is Shocking

Mrs. Rachel Lynde was a busybody who lived in Avonlea, a town on beautiful Prince Edward Island off Canada's Atlantic coast.

Now Avonlea occupied a little peninsula that jutted out, with water on both sides. It was impossible for any traveler on the hill road to pass in and out of town without Mrs. Rachel noticing. And notice she did! Every spare minute she had, she sat by her kitchen window knitting her "cotton warp" quilts and watching the comings and goings on the road.

One warm June afternoon, she was amazed

to see Matthew Cuthbert drive by. Not only was he using his buggy and sorrel mare, but he was wearing his best suit. All this led Mrs. Rachel to believe Matthew was traveling out of Avonlea—a fair distance, no doubt. Now where was Matthew Cuthbert going and why?

If it had been any other man in town, Mrs. Rachel would have known the answer to those questions. But Matthew was different from other folks. He was a shy man who never visited or ventured far from home. She felt certain that Matthew must be on an important mission.

"I'll just go over to Green Gables after tea and find out from Marilla what Matthew is up to," Mrs. Rachel muttered. "I want to get to the bottom of this mystery."

Green Gables, a large, rambling house set amid flowering orchards, was located a quarter mile up the road from Lynde's Hollow. When Mrs. Rachel arrived there later in the afternoon, Matthew's sister, Marilla, was sit-

He Was Wearing His Best Suit.

ting in her tidy kitchen knitting. Behind her, three plates were laid on the table.

Marilla must be expecting Matthew to bring someone home for tea, Mrs. Rachel thought. However, the dishes were everyday dishes and there were only crab apple preserves and one kind of cake. The company could not be anyone special. Yet what could explain Matthew's unusual appearance today?

"Good evening, Rachel," Marilla said. She was a tall, thin woman who wore her gray-streaked hair swept up in a bun on the back of her head. "Won't you sit down? How are all your folks?"

"We are all fine," Mrs. Rachel answered. "I was worried about you though, when I saw Matthew drive by earlier. I thought maybe he was going to get the doctor because you were ill."

"Oh, I'm quite well," Marilla told her, knowing full well how curious her nosy neighbor must be about Matthew's trip. "Matthew went

Expecting Someone for Tea

to Bright River. We are getting a little boy from an orphanage in Nova Scotia, and he's coming on the train tonight."

If Marilla had said that Matthew had gone to Bright River to meet a kangaroo from Australia, Mrs. Rachel could not have been more astonished. Nothing would ever surprise her again! Nothing! "What on earth put such a notion in your head, Marilla?" she demanded disapprovingly.

"We've been thinking of this all winter," Marilla said. "Mrs. Alexander Spencer was here before Christmas. She said she was going to get a little girl from the Hopeton orphanage in the spring. So Matthew and I decided to get a boy. We send word to Mrs. Spencer by her brother, Robert, to pick out someone about eleven who can help with the chores. Matthew is sixty years old now, and he's not as spry as he used to be. He has a slight heart condition, you know."

"Well, Marilla, I'll tell you right out I think

"He's Coming on the Train Tonight."

you're doing a risky thing. You're bringing a strange child into your house, and you don't know a thing about him. Why, only last week I read in the paper how a couple took in an orphan boy, and he set their house on fire. He nearly burned them to a crisp in their beds."

"I admit I've had some doubts myself, Rachel," Marilla told her neighbor, who was red in the face from her outburst. "But Matthew's mind was made up. I could see that, so I gave in."

"I hope it turns out all right," replied Mrs. Rachel anxiously. "Just the other day I heard about an orphan girl who put poison in her adopted family's well."

"We're not getting a girl," said Marilla, ignoring Mrs. Rachel's gloomy comment. "I'd never dream of raising a girl. So you see, Rachel, the matter is all settled."

Mrs. Rachel would have liked to stay at Green Gables until Matthew returned with his young charge, but that would have been a long

"I've Had Some Doubts Myself."

wait. She decided to drop by Robert Bell's house to tell this unbelievable news. It would certainly create sensations, and Mrs. Rachel loved to create a sensation. The truth was that Marilla was glad to see her leave.

"Well, of all things that ever were or will be," Mrs. Rachel said when she was safely out in the lane. "I'm sorry for that poor boy waiting at the station. Matthew and Marilla don't know anything about raising children. They will expect him to be wiser than his own grandfather. I just can't imagine a child at Green Gables! After all, there's never been one there before."

At the very moment she spoke those words, Matthew Cuthbert drove up to the Bright River station. At first he thought he was early. But the stationmaster told him the 5:30 train had come and gone. To his dismay, the young orphan boy he had come to meet was nowhere to be seen.

The only person in sight was a skinny, red-

"Imagine a Child at Green Gables!"

headed girl sitting straight and tall on a pile of shingles at the end of the station platform.

Matthew walked past her hurriedly, avoiding her gaze. Yet out of the corner of his eye, he could see that her hands were clasped tightly in front of her and that her body was tense and rigid. He had the feeling that this poor child was waiting anxiously for someone.

This Poor Child Was Waiting for Someone.

"A Passenger for You."

Chapter Two

A Difficult Homecoming

"There was a passenger dropped off for you," the stationmaster called out to Matthew. "That little girl sitting over there."

"I'm not expecting a girl," Matthew said nervously. Except for Marilla and Mrs. Rachel Lynde, women made him most uncomfortable. "I've come for a boy. Mrs. Alexander Spencer was to bring a boy over from Nova Scotia."

The stationmaster whistled. "Guess there's been some mistake. Mrs. Spencer got off with that girl and left her in my charge. Said you and your sister were adopting her and would be along for her soon."

For the first time, Matthew took a good look at the little waif who sat there on the shingles eyeing him. A freckle-faced child of about eleven, she was dressed in a short, drab yellow-grey dress and a faded brown sailor hat. Her bright red hair was plaited in two thick braids.

"I suppose you are Mr. Matthew Cuthbert of Green Gables," she piped up in a sweet voice. "I was beginning to fear you weren't coming for me. I had decided that if you didn't come tonight, I'd go down the track to that wild cherry tree and climb up in its white blossoms to sleep. I could imagine I was living in marble halls."

Matthew took her scrawny little hand in his. "I'm sorry I was late," he said shyly. He simply could not tell this child with the glowing eyes that there had been a mistake. Marilla would have to do that. "Come along," he said. "The horse is over in the yard. Give me your

Matthew Took a Good Look.

bag."

"Oh, I can carry it," the girl said cheerfully. "I'm so glad you've come. It seems so wonderful that I'm going to belong to you. I've never belonged to anybody before—not really."

Matthew and his charge reached the buggy and climbed in. As they left the village and made their way down a steep hill, they drove along a road fringed on either side with blooming wild cherry trees and white birches.

"Isn't this a beautiful sight?" his companion exclaimed. "What do these lacy white trees remind you of?"

"Well now, I dunno," Matthew replied.

"Why, a bride of course—all in white with a misty veil. I don't ever expect to be a bride because I'm too homely. But I have dreams of wearing pretty clothes someday. Why, only this morning I put on this ugly old dress and pretended it was a gorgeous blue silk gown. I was happy all the way over on the boat to Prince Edward Island. Oh, I never dreamed

Cherry Trees and White Birches

that I would get to live here. Tell me, why are all the roads red?"

"Well now, I dunno," Matthew answered.

"This is one of the things I shall have to find out," the newcomer said. "This is such an interesting world. It wouldn't be half as interesting if we knew all about everything, would it? Am I talking too much, Mr. Cuthbert? Mrs. Spencer says I do."

Much to his own surprise, Matthew was enjoying himself. Like most quiet folks, he liked talkative people, particularly this little girl who seemed to say the first thing that popped into her head. "Oh, you can talk as much as you like," he assured her. "I don't mind."

"Oh, I'm so glad," his new friend replied. "I know you and I are going to get along just fine."

As they drove the remainder of the eight miles to Green Gables, the young girl chatted on and on about the beautiful scenery.

At one point they drove through an archway

"Such an Interesting World."

ANNE OF GREEN GABLES

of fragrant apple blossoms. Enchanted by the sight, the girl whispered, "Oh, Mr. Cuthbert, what was that place we just passed through?"

"We call it The Avenue," Matthew told her.

"Oh, it was wonderful," she cried. "It gave me a funny, sort of pleasant ache inside. Did you ever have an ache like that?"

"Well, now, I don't know that I have."

"The name Avenue just doesn't properly describe that stretch of road," she blurted out. "I'm going to rename it the White Way of Delight."

They drove over the crest of a hill and gazed at the pond below, its water a glory of many different colors. A bridge spanned it midway.

"That's Barry's Pond," Matthew said. "It's named for Mr. Barry who lives at Orchard Slope over there. He has a daughter, Diana—about your age, I think."

"Oh, I don't like the name Barry's Pond either. I shall change it to the Lake of Shining Waters because the water looks as if it's smil-

"The White Way of Delight"

ing up at me."

"We're almost home now," Matthew interrupted, looking down at her shining little face.

"That's Green Gables over there in the distance."

It was dark when Matthew pulled into the lane at Green Gables. With a heavy heart he escorted the eager girl into the house.

"Matthew Cuthbert," cried Marilla, running into the front hall to greet them. "Where is the boy?"

"There wasn't any boy," Matthew stammered, putting down the girl's suitcase. "There was only her."

"But there must have been a boy," Marilla insisted. "Mrs. Spencer was supposed to bring us a boy. This is a pretty piece of business."

Suddenly their visitor realized the truth of the situation. "You don't want me," she cried, dropping into a chair and sobbing uncontrollably. "Nobody ever did want me! I might have known the dream was too beautiful to last."

"Where is the Boy?"

"There's no need to cry," Marilla said.

"Yes, there is," the girl wailed. "You would cry, too, if you were an orphan and had come to a new home only to learn no one wanted you because you weren't a boy."

"Come now. Stop crying. You will spend the night with us, and then we'll investigate this matter tomorrow. What is your name?" Marilla asked.

"Will you please call me Cordelia?" the girl asked.

"Is that your name?" Marilla wanted to know.

"No," the girl admitted, "but I would like to be called Cordelia. It's such an elegant name."

"What is your real name?" Marilla asked.

"Anne Shirley," the girl replied. "Oh, why didn't you tell me at the station that you didn't want me, Mr. Cuthbert? If I hadn't seen the White Way of Delight and the Lake of Shining Waters, this wouldn't be so hard."

"What on earth does she mean?" Marilla

"You Would Cry Too."

asked, staring at Matthew.

"She's just referring to some conversation we had on our way here. Now, don't you think it's time we ate dinner?"

The three of them sat down at the dinner table, but Anne just picked at her food. "I can't eat," she told Matthew and Marilla. "I am in the depths of despair."

"I guess she's tired," Matthew said. "I think you better put her to bed, Marilla."

After Marilla tucked the tearful girl into bed in the east gable room, she had a long talk with Matthew in the kitchen.

"I will drive over to see Mrs. Alexander Spencer tomorrow," Marilla announced as she began washing the dishes. "That girl will have to be sent back to the orphanage."

"Yes, I suppose so," Matthew said quietly.

"You suppose so! Don't you know it?" Marilla fairly shouted.

"Well now, Marilla. She's a real nice little thing, and she does want to stay with us," he

But Anne Just Picked at Her Food.

said.

"What good would she be to us?" his sister asked.

"We might be some good to her," Matthew said unexpectedly.

"Matthew, this child has bewitched you. It's plain as plain you want to keep her," Marilla said.

"You should have heard her talk on the way over here," Matthew persisted. "She's a real interesting little thing."

"Look, Matthew," Marilla said. "I don't want an orphan girl, and if I did, I wouldn't want her. And that is my final word."

"What Good Would She Be?"

The Glorious World of Green Gables

Chapter Three

Marilla Is in a Dilemma

The next morning was a beautiful, warm June day drenched in sunshine. Anne simply refused to waste one minute being unhappy.

She jumped out of bed and threw open the windows and gazed in awe at the glorious world of Green Gables. An apple orchard bloomed on one side of the house and a cherry grove on the other. In the distance, fields of grass were sprinkled with dandelions and clover. Gardens blossomed with fragrant lilacs, and a brook meandered lazily through the property. Off to the left, Anne spotted two big barns, and on the horizon she glimpsed the sparkling blue sea.

"What a lovely place," she murmured. "I could imagine living here forever."

At breakfast she told Marilla she didn't dare go outside. "If I go outside and explore Green Gables, I won't be able to stop loving it. It's hard enough now, and I don't want to make it any harder. I know you don't want to keep me because I'm not a boy."

"I never in all my life saw or heard anything to equal her," muttered Marilla, beating a retreat down the cellar stairs after potatoes. "She will say just anything! First thing you know, she'll be casting a spell over me, too."

Late in the afternoon a determined Marilla took Anne in the buggy to visit Mrs. Alexander Spencer in White Sands and straighten out the misunderstanding that had occurred.

"I'm sure Mrs. Spencer will make arrangements to send Anne back to the orphanage," she said to Matthew as she drove off. It was

On the Way to White Sands

hard to ignore the wistful expression on his face.

"I've made up my mind to enjoy the trip," Anne said as they rode along. "I'm not going to think about returning to the orphanage. I'm just going to think about the drive. Are we going across the Lake of Shining Waters today?"

"We're not going over Barry's Pond if that's what you mean by your Lake of Shining Waters," Marilla said. "We're going along the shore road. Since it's five miles to White Sands, why don't you use this time to tell me about yourself—not your imaginings—but the facts."

"I am eleven years old," Anne began. "I was born in Bolingbroke, Nova Scotia to Walter and Bertha Shirley. My father was a high school teacher, but they were very poor and died of the fever when I was only four months old. Since there were no relatives nearby, a Mrs. Thomas took me. But she was poor, too,

"I Am Eleven Years Old," Anne Began.

and had a drunken husband. I lived with them until I was eight. When Mr. Thomas died, his mother gave Mrs. Thomas and the kids a home. But she didn't want me."

"I see," said Marilla quietly. "Who did you live with after that?"

"A Mrs. Hammond from up the river," Anne explained. "She needed someone to help with her twins. She had three sets, you see. When her husband died, the family was split up. I was sent to that awful orphanage where I lived for four months until Mrs. Spencer came and picked me."

"Were those women—Mrs. Thomas and Mrs. Hammond—good to you?" asked Marilla, looking at Anne out of the corner of her eye.

"Oh," faltered Anne sadly. "They meant to be. They had a lot to worry them, you know. It's very hard to have a drunken husband and twins three times. But I'm sure they meant to be."

What a sad, unhappy life this child has had,

"Were Those Women Good to You?"

Marilla thought. No wonder she was so delighted at the prospect of a real home. Maybe I *should* indulge Matthew's whim and let her stay. I must say she's very ladylike and nice. She talks too much, but she could be trained out of that.

When they arrived at Mrs. Spencer's big yellow house in White Sands, she seemed surprised to see them. "Dear, dear," she exclaimed. "You're the last folks I was looking for today. But I'm real glad to see you."

"I'm afraid a mistake has been made, and I've come to get to the bottom of it," Marilla stated. "Matthew and I sent you word by your brother to bring us a boy from the orphanage."

"Marilla Cuthbert, you don't say," cried Mrs. Spencer in distress. "Why, Robert sent word down by his daughter, Nancy, and she said that you wanted a girl, didn't he, Flora Jean?" She turned and looked intently at her daughter who had come to the steps.

"She certainly did, Miss Cuthbert," Flora

Mrs. Spencer's Big Yellow House

Jean answered earnestly.

"I'm dreadfully sorry," said Mrs. Spencer. "It's too bad, but it wasn't my fault. I thought I was following your instructions."

"It was our own fault," Marilla said. "We should not have allowed an important message to be passed along by word of mouth. Can we send this child back to the orphanage?"

"Yes, you can, but I don't think that will be necessary," Mrs. Spencer informed her. "Mrs. Peter Blewett was here yesterday wishing for a little girl to help her with her large family. Anne would be the perfect child for her."

Marilla knew she should be grateful for the opportunity to get this unwelcome orphan off her hands, but for some reason this news was very unsettling. Mrs. Blewett had a reputation for having a bad temper and a stingy nature. Her children were supposed to be very naughty, too.

"This is your lucky day," exclaimed Mrs. Spencer. "Here is Mrs. Blewett coming up the

"Can We Send This Child Back?"

lane now. Why don't all of you move into the parlor and have a seat? You take the armchair, Miss Cuthbert, and you sit on the ottoman, Anne, but don't wiggle. Flora Jean, you go put the buns in the oven."

Mrs. Blewett stormed into the room and plopped down on the sofa.

"Good afternoon, Mrs. Blewett," Mrs. Spencer said. "We just were saying how fortunate it was you happened along. Let me introduce you to Miss Cuthbert and Anne Shirley."

Anne sat mutely on the ottoman with her hands clasped tightly in her lap, staring at Mrs. Blewett. Was she really going to have to live with this sharp-faced, sharp-eyed woman? She felt a lump in her throat and tears stinging her eyes.

"It seems there's been a mistake about this little girl, Mrs. Blewett," Mrs. Spencer explained. "I was under the impression that Mr. and Miss Cuthbert wanted to adopt a girl. I was certainly told so. But it seems it was a boy

Mrs. Blewett Stormed Into the Room.

they wanted. So if you still would like to have a girl, Anne would be just the one for you."

"Humph. You don't look like there's much to you," Mrs. Blewett barked at Anne. "If I take you, you will have to earn your keep. I need a lot of help with the new baby. He cries all the time. I'm just clean worn out taking care of him."

Marilla looked at Anne's pale face and rose to her feet. "Just a minute, Mrs. Blewett. Before you say another word, I have an announcement to make."

Marilla Rose to Her Feet.

"It'll Have to," Mrs. Blewett Snapped.

Chapter Four

Anne Learns Marilla's Decision

"I have decided to take Anne home overnight and talk this situation over with Matthew again," Marilla said slowly. "After all, I never said we wouldn't keep Anne. I just came here to find out how the mistake was made. If we make up our minds not to keep her, we'll bring her over to you tomorrow night, Mrs. Blewett. If we don't, you know Anne is going to stay with us. Will that suit you?"

"I suppose it'll have to," Mrs. Blewett snapped.

During Marilla's speech, Anne's eyes grew

deep and bright as morning stars. When Mrs. Spencer and Mrs. Blewett went out to the kitchen, she flew to Marilla's side. "Oh, Miss Cuthbert, did you really say that perhaps you would let me stay at Green Gables?" she whispered. "Or did I only imagine that you did?"

"I think you better learn to control your imagination, Anne, so you know what's real and what isn't," Marilla answered crossly. "Yes, you did hear me say that and no more. It isn't decided yet, and perhaps we will let Mrs. Blewett take you. After all, she certainly needs you more than I do."

"I'd rather go back to the orphanage than go live with her," Anne cried. "She looks like . . . like . . . a real shrew!"

"You should be ashamed of yourself for talking badly about a lady like Mrs. Blewett," Marilla replied, smothering a smile. "Come along, Anne. We must go home."

When they arrived back at Green Gables that evening, Matthew met them in the lane.

"Perhaps You'll Let Me Stay?"

He seemed relieved to see that Anne had returned.

Later when they were behind the barn milking cows, Marilla told him about Anne's tragic past and the results of her interview with Mrs. Spencer.

"I wouldn't give a dog to that Blewett woman," Matthew said vehemently.

"Well, I certainly agree with you, Matthew. But it's either Mrs. Blewett or us. Since you seem so set on taking Anne, I guess I'm willing. I've never brought up a child, especially a girl, but I'll do my best."

Matthew's face glowed with delight. "Well, Marilla, I reckoned you'd come to see it that way. She's such an interesting little thing."

"I'd be much happier if you could say she was a useful thing," retorted Marilla. "But I'll make it my business to train her to be. And mind you, Matthew, you're not to interfere with my methods. Maybe an old maid doesn't know much about raising a child, but she

Behind the Barn

knows more than an old bachelor. So you just let me manage her."

"Have it your way, Marilla," Matthew said. "Only be as good and kind to her as you can without spoiling her. I really think you could do anything with her if you got her to love you."

Marilla didn't tell Anne that they had decided to keep her until the next afternoon. All that morning she kept her busy doing various chores and observed her progress. By noon she had concluded that Anne was bright and obedient, willing to work and quick to learn. Her only fault seemed to be her tendency to daydream on the job.

When Anne had finished the lunch dishes, she suddenly confronted Marilla. "Oh, Miss Cuthbert, I've been patient all morning, but I really must know if you're going to send me away."

"Well," said Marilla, "I suppose I might as well tell you that Matthew and I have decided

Her Tendency to Daydream

to keep you, that is, if you will try to be a good girl. Why, child, whatever is the matter?"

"I'm crying," said a bewildered Anne. "I can't think why. I'm glad as glad can be. But glad isn't quite the right word. I was glad about the White Way and the cherry blossoms. But now I'm more than glad. I'm so happy. It will be up-hill work to be good. Mrs. Thomas often told me I was desperately wicked. But can you tell me why I'm crying?"

"I suppose it's because you're so excited," Marilla said. "Now sit down and try to relax. We are going to try and raise you right. First of all, I want you to go to Sunday School and learn your prayers. You can start this afternoon by memorizing the Lord's Prayer. And secondly, you will go to elementary school in the fall. And one more thing, I want you to call me Marilla and not Miss Cuthbert."

"Oh, this is all so wonderful," Anne cried. "I could pretend I was Lady Cordelia all dressed up in a gown of white lace with a pearl cross

"Glad as Glad Can Be"

on my chest and pearls in my hair. But no, I am Anne of Green Gables, and that is so much better than being Anne of anywhere. Oh, and I do so want to have a best friend here in Avonlea. Do you think that is possible, Marilla?"

"Maybe so," Marilla answered thoughtfully. "Diana Barry lives over at Orchard Slope and she's about your age. Right now she's away visiting her aunt in Carmody. But hopefully you will get acquainted when she returns. In the meantime, you'll be meeting some of my friends."

Mrs. Rachel Lynde was the first person in Avonlea to come to Green Gables to meet Anne. When Mrs. Rachel arrived, Anne was outside on one of her many exploring trips around the farm.

"It was too bad a mistake was made about the adoption," Mrs. Rachel told Marilla. "Couldn't you have sent the girl back?"

"Yes," Marilla replied. "But Matthew had taken a fancy to her, and I grew to like her, too.

"I Am Anne of Green Gables."

This house is a different place now that she's here. Oh, look, Rachel, here comes Anne now."

"Well, they didn't pick you for your looks," Mrs. Rachel said when Anne came flying in the door. "What a skinny, homely girl you are! Did you ever see such freckles and bright red hair?"

"You are a rude, nasty woman and fat, too!" Anne screamed, stamping her foot on the floor. "I hate you, Mrs. Rachel. I hate you!" She burst into tears and fled from the room.

"They Didn't Pick You for Your Looks."

"I Don't Envy You."

Chapter Five

The Apology

"Well, I don't envy you your job of bringing up that girl, Marilla," said Mrs. Rachel, glaring indignantly at her friend.

"You shouldn't have ridiculed her about her looks, Rachel," Marilla answered, amazed at her own response.

"Marilla Cuthbert, you aren't defending her after that terrible display of temper, are you?"

"No," said Marilla slowly. "She's been naughty, and I will have to talk to her about it. But she's never been taught what's right. And you were too hard on her, Rachel."

"Well, I can see that I'll have to be very careful what I say after this since the feelings of orphans have to be considered before anything else. I'll be on my way now. Don't expect me to come hurrying back here though."

When Mrs. Rachel finally left, Marilla rushed up to the east gable room where she found Anne facedown on the bed crying bitterly.

"Anne," she said, "get off that bed this minute. That was a nice way for you to behave! Why did you have to insult Mrs. Rachel Lynde of all people?"

"She hadn't any right to call me ugly and red-headed," wailed Anne.

"You didn't have any right to fly into such a rage and talk the way you did to her. I was ashamed of you," said Marilla.

"Just imagine how you'd feel if somebody told you that you were skinny and ugly," pleaded Anne tearfully.

"It's true Rachel is much too frank," Marilla

Anne Was Crying Bitterly.

said in a softer tone. "But she was a stranger, an older person, and my visitor—all three good reasons for you to be respectful of her. You simply must apologize and ask her to forgive you."

"I could never do that," said a determined Anne. "You can punish me any way you like. You can shut me up in a dark, damp dungeon inhabited by snakes and toads and feed me only bread and water, but I will not ask Mrs. Rachel to forgive me."

"I guess I won't put you in a dungeon," said Marilla. "But apologize you must. You'll stay here in your room until you change your mind."

"I shall stay here forever then," said Anne mournfully. "I can't tell Mrs. Rachel I'm sorry when I'm not. I can't even imagine that I'm sorry."

"Perhaps your imagination will be working better in the morning," said Marilla, rising to leave. "You will have the night to think over your conduct and change your mind."

"Punish Me Any Way You Like."

When Anne stayed stubbornly in her room during breakfast, Marilla had to tell Matthew the whole story.

"It's a good thing Rachel Lynde got a talking to. She's a meddlesome old gossip," Matthew said.

"Matthew, I'm surprised at you. You know Anne's behavior was dreadful, and yet you take her part. Do you think she shouldn't be punished at all?" Marilla asked.

"I reckon she ought to be punished a little," Matthew conceded. "But don't be too hard on her."

Despite the fact Marilla carried Anne's meals to her room on a tray, the girl ate very little, and she didn't leave the room.

That evening when Marilla went out to bring the cows back from the pasture, Matthew slipped in the house and crept upstairs. He tiptoed down the hall and stood for a few minutes outside the east gable room. Then he opened the door and peeked in.

Marilla Had to Tell Matthew.

Anne was sitting by the window looking very small and unhappy. Softly Matthew closed the door and went over to her. "How are you doing, Anne?" he whispered.

"Pretty well. I imagine a great deal, and that helps pass the time," she said.

"Don't you think you'd better apologize to Mrs. Rachel Lynde and get it over with? You know how determined Marilla is about this."

"I admit that I have calmed down overnight, and I am sorry now," Anne said sweetly. "I suppose I could apologize for you. Do you really want me to?"

"Of course I do. It's terribly lonesome downstairs without you. Just go and smooth it over—that's a good girl. But don't tell Marilla I said a word. She might think I was interfering, and I promised I wouldn't." With that, Matthew fled hastily outdoors to the remotest corner of the cow pasture.

When Marilla returned to the house, Anne announced that she was ready to make the

Matthew Went Over to Her.

apology.

Mrs. Rachel was knitting by her kitchen window when her visitors arrived on their important mission. "Come on in," she called.

Once inside, Anne fell to her knees and cried, "Oh, Mrs. Rachel, I'm extremely sorry. I behaved terribly to you, and I've disgraced my dear friends, Matthew and Marilla. It was very wicked of me to fly into a temper because you told me the truth. My hair is red, and I'm freckled and skinny and ugly. Oh, Mrs. Rachel, please forgive me."

Mrs. Rachel didn't notice that Anne was putting on a performance and enjoying every minute of it. "There, there, child. Of course I forgive you. I guess I am a terribly outspoken person. You mustn't mind me. You know I went to school with a girl with bright red hair like yours. When she grew up, her hair turned a handsome auburn color. I wouldn't be surprised if yours did, too—not a bit."

"Oh, Mrs. Rachel," Anne said in a long

Their Important Mission

breath as she rose to her feet. "You have given me real hope. I shall always consider you my benefactor and friend. I could endure anything if only I thought my hair would be a handsome auburn when I grow up."

"I apologized pretty well, didn't I?" Anne asked Marilla on the way home. She bent over to smell the white narcissi Mrs. Rachel had given her when they said good-bye.

"You did it quite thoroughly," Marilla agreed, secretly amused. "I hope you will try to control your temper in the future."

"That wouldn't be hard if people wouldn't tease me about my looks and make me mad," Anne remarked with a sigh.

"You shouldn't worry so much about your looks. Pretty is as pretty does," Marilla reminded her.

Far up in the shadows a light gleamed out through the trees from the kitchen at Green Gables. Suddenly, Anne slipped her hand into Marilla's. "It's lovely to be going home and

On the Way Home

know it's home," she said. "Marilla, I'm so happy."

Something warm and pleasant welled up in Marilla's heart at the touch of Anne's hand—a feeling of motherhood she had missed until now.

"Hurry along, Anne," the older woman urged. "I have a surprise waiting for you at Green Gables."

A Surprise Waiting at Green Gables

"How Do You Like Them?"

Chapter Six

The Joy of a New Friendship

"How do you like them?" asked Marilla.

Anne was standing in the gable room looking down at three new dresses spread out on the bed. One was a dreary brown gingham. Another was a black-and-white checked sateen, and the third was a stiff print in an ugly blue shade. Marilla had made the dresses herself, and they were all extremely plain.

"I'll try to imagine that I like them," said Anne slowly.

"You don't like them. I can tell," Marilla replied, offended. "What's wrong with them?"

"They're—they're not—pretty," said Anne slowly, trying not to hurt Marilla's feelings.

"Pretty!" Marilla cried. "I didn't go to all that trouble just to make pretty dresses for you. Those are good, sensible gowns that I expect you to take good care of. I should think you'd be grateful after all those skimpy things you've been wearing."

"But I am grateful," insisted Anne. "But I'd be ever so much gratefuller if—if you'd make just one with puffed sleeves. They're so fashionable."

"I think puffed sleeves are ridiculous looking," Marilla replied, looking down at her own simple dress. "I prefer plain, sensible sleeves."

"But I'd rather look ridiculous with everybody else than plain and sensible all by myself," persisted Anne sadly.

"I expect you to hang up those dresses carefully and then sit down and learn your Sunday lesson. Tomorrow will be your first day," was Marilla's only reply as she marched out the

"They're—They're Not—Pretty."

door.

The next morning Marilla had a bad headache, so Anne set off on her own for church, wearing the stiff black-and-white sateen dress and a plain, flat sailor hat. At the main road, she picked some buttercups and wild pink roses and adorned her hat with a heavy wreath of them.

Unfortunately, Anne had a miserable time at Sunday School and church. All the girls, who were dressed in pastel-colored dresses with puffed sleeves, stared at her flower-laden hat and began whispering and giggling behind her back. Not one person came up to her to say hello.

To make matters worse, Miss Rogerson, her Sunday School teacher, Mr. Bell who gave the opening prayer, and Mr. Bentley who delivered the sermon, were all long-winded and dull. When Anne came home very dejected, Marilla had to admit that some of her complaints were true.

She Picked Buttercups and Roses.

Gossip about Anne and her funny hat filtered back to Marilla by the next Friday. Mrs. Rachel Lynde wasted no time in making sure she knew that Anne had not made a good impression at church. Although Marilla was embarrassed, she took steps to get Anne's mind off the unpleasant incident.

"Cheer up, Anne," Marilla said. "I've got some good news for you. Diana Barry came home today. I'm going to see if I can borrow a skirt pattern from Mrs. Barry. Why don't you come along and meet Diana?"

"Oh, Marilla, I'm scared. What if she doesn't like me?" Anne asked, suddenly tensing inside.

"I'm sure Diana will like you just fine," Marilla assured her. "It's her mother you have to reckon with. If she has heard about your outburst with Mrs. Rachel and the buttercup bedecked hat you wore to church, I don't know what she'll think of you. You better be very polite and well-behaved. Let's be on our way

"What If She Doesn't Like Me?"

now."

They went over to Orchard Slope, taking a short cut across a brook and up the fir-covered hill grove.

Mrs. Barry came to the kitchen door and invited them in. "This is my daughter, Diana," she said, ushering her guests into the living room.

Diana, a pretty little girl with her mother's black eyes and hair, was sitting on the sofa reading a book. "Hello," she said, smiling.

"Diana, you might take Anne out in the garden and show her your flowers. Diana reads entirely too much," Mrs. Barry added to Marilla as the girls left the room.

Outside in the garden Anne and Diana stared at each other over a clump of orange tiger lilies.

"Oh, Diana," said Anne suddenly, clasping her hands and speaking almost in a whisper, "do you think you could like me a little—enough to be my best friend?"

Diana Was on the Sofa Reading.

"Why, I guess I could," Diana said. "I'm really awfully glad you've come to Green Gables. It will be wonderful to have someone to play with."

"Do you swear to be my best friend forever?" demanded Anne.

"It's dreadfully wicked to swear, you know," said Diana.

"You don't have to say any bad words," Anne softened her request. "All you have to do is take a solemn vow."

"I don't mind doing that," Diana replied, much relieved. "How do we do it?"

"We must join hands," Anne said gravely. "And we should do it over water. We'll just pretend that this path is running water. I'll take my oath first. I do solemnly swear to be faithful to my best friend, Diana Barry, as long as the sun and moon shall endure. Now you take your vow and use my name."

Diana repeated the oath, and the two new friends parted with many promises to spend

"Do You Swear?"

the next afternoon together.

"I'm the happiest girl on Prince Edward Island," Anne confided to Marilla on the way home. "Diana and I are going to build a playhouse in Mr. William Bell's birch grove tomorrow. Can I have those broken pieces of china that are out in the woodshed? Diana is going to show me a place back in the woods where rice lilies grow, and she is going to teach me to sing a song called 'Nelly in the Hazel Dell'," she added after taking a deep breath.

"I do hope that you won't talk Diana to death," said Marilla. "Please remember when you make your plans that you have your work to do. It'll have to be done before you play with Diana."

The days that followed were a happy time for Anne. She spent endless hours playing make-believe games with Diana in their woodland house they named Idlewild. As the friendship between the two girls flourished, Matthew and Marilla were delighted to see

The Happiest Girl on Prince Edward Island

how generous and kind their Anne was to her friend.

One night as Marilla sat darning socks in the sitting room with Matthew, she expressed a deep concern she had about her new daughter. "Anne's really a wonderful girl, but she is different. I do hope she's going to fit in with the other children at school when it opens in September," she said. "I do so want her to be happy."

She Expressed a Deep Concern.

"I'm Dreadfully Behind."

Chapter Seven

A Stormy Encounter at School

Despite Marilla's misgivings, Anne got off to a good start. "I think I'm going to really like school here in Avonlea," she told Marilla after the first day. "I get to sit with Diana right by the window, so we can look out and see the Lake of Shining Water. There are a lot of nice girls at school, but of course I like Diana best."

"How did you like your courses?" Marilla asked.

"I'm dreadfully behind, I'm afraid," Anne said frankly. "I'll have to work hard to catch up. Mr. Phillips, our teacher—I don't like him too much—already started us on reading, spelling, geography, and Canadian history. That I did like."

So it was that the first three weeks of school sailed quickly by. At the end of September, Gilbert Blythe, who had been visiting his cousins in New Brunswick all summer, returned to Avonlea and joined his class.

Diana explained to Anne that Gilbert, a handsome young boy with curly brown hair, hazel eyes, and a dazzling smile, had a reputation for being a terrible tease. As luck would have it, he sat right across the aisle from Anne.

The first day Gilbert was back, Anne glanced over and was shocked to see him pin the long yellow braid of Ruby Gillis, who sat in front of him, to the back of her seat. When Ruby got up, she fell back into her chair with a shriek, thinking her hair had been pulled out at the roots. Mr. Phillips glared at her so sternly that poor Ruby began to cry. Gilbert looked

Anne Was Shocked.

over at Anne and winked.

"I think your Gilbert Blythe is very handsome," Anne confided to Diana later, "but he has a lot of nerve. Imagine him winking at me—a complete stranger."

That afternoon Mr. Philips was in a corner explaining an algebra problem to Prissy Andrews, while the rest of the class were doing pretty much as they pleased. Gilbert Blythe tried repeatedly to get Anne's attention, but she was lost in an exciting daydream.

Now Gilbert was not used to a girl ignoring him. He reached across the aisle, picked up the end of Anne's long red braid, held it at arm's length, and whispered loudly, "Carrots! Carrots!"

Enraged, Anne sprang to her feet and exclaimed, "Gilbert, you mean, hateful boy! How dare you talk to me like that!" And then— thwack! She picked up her slate and cracked it over the astonished boy's head.

"Oh," everyone said in horrified delight.

And Then—Thwack!

Diana gasped. Ruby Gillis, who was inclined to be hysterical anyway, began to cry.

A red-faced Mr. Phillips stalked quickly down the aisle. "Anne Shirley, what is the meaning of this outburst?" he demanded.

"It was my fault, Mr. Phillips. I teased her," Gilbert said before Anne could utter a word.

But Mr. Phillips completely ignored Gilbert's remark. "I'm sorry to see a student of mine display such a temper and mean spirit," he said in a solemn tone. "Anne, go stand on the platform in front of the blackboard for the rest of the afternoon."

Above her head he wrote, "Anne Shirley has a very bad temper. Anne Shirley must learn to control her temper."

Anne stood on the platform till school was over, still furious with Gilbert Blythe. Not only did she refuse to accept the apology he made on the way out, but she told Diana she would never forgive him.

"You mustn't mind Gilbert for making fun of

Mr. Phillips Stalked Quickly Down the Aisle.

your hair," Diana said soothingly. "Why, he pokes fun at all the girls. He laughs at my hair because it's so black and calls me a crow all the time."

"There's a big difference between being called a crow and being called carrots," Anne insisted. "Gilbert Blythe has hurt my feelings excruciatingly, Diana."

The entire matter might have blown over if nothing else had happened. However, the next day at lunch time the students were picking gum in Mr. Bell's spruce grove as they often did. Usually they were careful to keep an eye open for Mr. Phillips who lived nearby, so they could hurry back to school before he did.

Unfortunately, this particular day the boys and girls lingered too long in the grove and made it back to school just seconds after the the teacher. Anne, her hair wreathed with lilies, had been dancing alone in the woods like a sprite. Arms flying, she dashed into class the last one.

Mr. Bell's Spruce Grove

Since Mr. Phillips didn't want to punish a dozen tardy students, he chose Anne. "Take those silly flowers out of your hair and go sit with Gilbert Blythe," he ordered. "Did you hear me?"

Anne rose haughtily, stepped across the aisle, and sat down beside Gilbert Blythe. Then she buried her face in her arms on the desk for the rest of the afternoon. To Anne, this was the end. It was bad enough to be singled out for punishment from among a dozen equally guilty classmates, but worse to be forced to sit with Gilbert. Never had she felt such shame.

When school was over, Anne removed everything from her desk—books, writing tablet, pen and ink—and stacked them on her cracked slate.

"Why are you taking these things home, Anne?" asked Diana as soon as they were out on the road.

"I'm not going back to school, that's why!"

She Buried Her Face in Her Arms.

Anne exclaimed.

Diana gasped. "Will Marilla let you stay home?"

"She'll have to," Anne said. "I'll never go back to school or to that man again!"

"I'll Never Go Back to School!"

"Humor Anne a Little."

Chapter Eight

Anne's Tea Party Is a Disaster

When Anne announced her decision not to go back to school, Marilla tried everything in her power to persuade her differently. She even consulted her friend, Mrs. Rachel Lynde, who had raised ten children.

Mrs. Rachel had heard the whole story from Tillie Boulter. Apparently all the students rather liked Anne and had taken her side.

"My advice to you," said Mrs. Rachel, who loved to give advice, "is to humor Anne a little. After all, it sounds like Mr. Phillips was in the wrong."

"Then you really think I'd better let her stay home?" asked Marilla in amazement.

"Yes," Mrs. Rachel replied. "I wouldn't mention school to Anne again until she brings it up. Depend upon it, Marilla, she'll cool off in about a week and will go back to school on her own. If you were to force her, dear knows what tantrum she'd throw, and you'd have more trouble than ever."

Marilla decided to follow Mrs. Rachel's advice and busy herself with her own affairs. "I'm going to a meeting of the Ladies' Aid Society in Carmody this afternoon," she told Anne one morning. "Why don't you invite Diana over for tea?"

"Oh, Marilla," Anne exclaimed. "How perfectly lovely. I see you are learning to imagine things, too, or else you'd never have understood how I've longed for this very thing. Can I use the rosebud spray tea set?"

"The rosebud spray tea set! Well, what next? You know I never use that except on special oc-

"How Perfectly Lovely."

casions. You'll use the old brown tea set. But you can open up that crock of cherry preserves and cut some fruitcake, too."

"Can we sit in the parlor?" Anne asked.

"No, the sitting room will do for you and your company. You might like that raspberry cordial from the last church social. It's on the second shelf of the closet." And Marilla left.

The afternoon tea was held began in a very grand, formal manner. Diana arrived at the front door right on time, and Anne ushered her into the sitting room where they chatted like ladies.

Diana told Anne how much everyone at school missed her and wished she'd come back. Then she related all the news about their classmates. However, when she mentioned Gilbert Blythe's name, Anne jumped up and suggested they have some raspberry cordial.

Anne looked on the second shelf of the closet but didn't see the bottle there. Finally she spied it on the top shelf, put it on a tray, and

Anne Suggested Some Cordial.

set it on the table with a tumbler. "Now, please help yourself, Diana," she urged. "I'll wait awhile because I had some apple juice before you came."

"My, this raspberry cordial is delicious," Diana exclaimed, drinking one glass and pouring herself a second. "Marilla certainly is a good cook."

"Yes, she is," Anne agreed. "Now she's trying to teach me to be a good cook and hostess, but I'm afraid I'm a great trial to her. Last Tuesday we had some plum pudding and sauce left over after dinner. Marilla asked me to set it in the pantry and cover it. Only I forgot until the next morning. You can imagine my horror in finding that a mouse had drowned in the pudding sauce."

"Oh my," cried Diana, pouring herself a third glass of raspberry cordial. "What did you do?"

"I lifted the mouse out of the sauce with a spoon and threw it out in the yard. I meant to

"My, This is Delicious."

tell Marilla about it, but I forgot. Then that night she had Mr. and Mrs. Charles Ross to dinner. Everything went smoothly until dessert when Marilla walked into the dining room with the plum pudding and warmed up sauce. I stood up and shrieked, 'Marilla, you mustn't serve that pudding sauce. I forgot to tell you a mouse drowned in it.' Marilla turned red as fire, carried the pudding and sauce out, and brought in some strawberries. Later she gave me a terrible scolding. Why, Diana, what is the matter?" she added, staring at her friend.

Diana stood up unsteadily. Then she sat down again, putting her hands to her head. "I'm awfully sick," she said thickly. "I must go home."

"But you haven't had your tea," Anne said, "or the fruitcake or cherry preserves."

"I must go home," Diana repeated. "I'm terribly dizzy."

With a heavy heart, Anne walked with

"I Must Go Home."

Diana as far as the Barrys' yard fence where they said good-bye. Anne's elegant tea party was over. On Monday Marilla sent Anne to Mrs. Rachel's on an errand. It wasn't long before Anne, tears streaming down her face, came flying home. "Mrs. Rachel was at Orchard Slope today and said Mrs. Barry was fit to be tied. She says I got Diana drunk and that she's never going to let her play with me again. All I gave her was the raspberry cordial."

"Drunk fiddlesticks!" said Marilla, marching to the sitting room closet. There on the shelf sat a bottle of her homemade currant wine. Suddenly she remembered that she had stored the raspberry cordial in the basement, not the sitting room, as she had told Anne.

Marilla went back to the kitchen with the wine bottle in her hand. "Anne, you have a genius for getting into trouble. You gave Diana the currant wine instead of the cordial. Didn't you know the difference?"

"I never tasted it," said Anne. "I thought I

"Fiddlesticks!"

was serving the cordial. I was just trying to be hospitable. I would never deliberately get my best friend drunk."

Despite the fact that both Marilla and Anne visited Orchard Slope and tried to impress upon Mrs. Barry that Anne had made an innocent mistake, the obstinate woman refused to listen. She remained absolutely firm in her decision that Diana could never play with Anne again.

The following Monday Anne surprised Marilla by returning to school. "School is all that's left for me in life now that Diana and I have parted company," she explained.

Anne was welcomed back to school with open arms. She flung herself into her studies and made rapid progress. A tremendous rivalry developed between Anne and Gilbert Blythe, who was as good-natured about it as Anne was intense. By the end of the term they were both promoted to the fifth grade.

One by one the months slipped slowly by.

With Open Arms

One cold January night when Marilla and Mrs. Rachel had gone to Charlottetown to hear a speech by the Canadian premier, Anne and Matthew were reading together at the kitchen table.

Suddenly they heard the sound of flying footsteps on the icy walk outside, and the next moment the kitchen door flew open. In rushed Diana Barry white-faced and breathless.

"Oh Anne," she cried. "My sister is desperately ill with croup, and Mother and Father are away. Do come quick. I'm scared to death!"

"I'm Scared to Death!"

"The Doctors Are Both Away."

Chapter Nine

A Happy Reunion

Without a word Matthew reached for his cap and coat, slipped past Diana, and rushed outside into the dark night.

"He's gone to harness the sorrel mare to go to Carmody for the doctor," said Anne, quickly putting on her jacket. "Matthew and I are such kindred spirits that I can read his thoughts."

"I don't believe he'll find any doctors in Carmody," sobbed Diana. "I think they're both away in Charlottetown. And Mary Joe, our nanny, doesn't know anything about croup."

"Don't cry, Di," said Anne to cheer her up. "I know exactly what to do for croup. Don't forget that Mrs. Hammond had twins three times, and they all had croup regularly. Just wait till I get that ipecac bottle. Come on now."

When they reached Orchard Slope, Anne took one look at Diana's three year old sister, Minny May, and saw she was terribly sick. Feverish and restless, she lay on the kitchen sofa breathing hoarsely. Young Mary Joe, a broad-faced French girl Mrs. Barry had hired to care for the children, was completely bewildered.

Without wasting a minute, Anne went right to work. "Minny May has croup all right," she declared. "She's pretty sick, but I've seen worse. First we have to have lots of hot water. Mary Joe, you put some wood on the stove. I'll undress Minny May and put her to bed. You find some soft flannel cloths, Diana. I'm going to give this poor child a dose of ipecac right away."

"I've Seen Worse."

Although Minny May resisted the medicine, Anne persuaded her to take it—not only once but many times during the long anxious night. It was three o'clock in the morning when Matthew arrived with the doctor he had summoned from Spencervale. By that time Minny May was greatly improved and sleeping soundly.

"I almost gave up on Minny May, doctor," Anne confessed. "At one point it looked like she might choke to death. But when I gave her that last dose of medicine, it did the trick. You can imagine my relief. After all, there are some things that can't be expressed in words."

"Yes, I know," nodded the doctor. He was looking at Anne as if he was thinking some things that couldn't be expressed in words, either.

Later on, however, he made his sentiments known to Mr. and Mrs. Barry. "That little red-headed girl over at Green Gables is as smart as they come. I tell you she saved Minny May's

"I Almost Gave Up," Anne Confessed.

life, for it would have been too late by the time I got there."

Anne walked home on that wonderful white-faced winter morning exhausted from lack of sleep. She crawled right into bed. When she awoke, she crept downstairs and found Marilla knitting in the kitchen.

"Did you see the premier?" asked Anne at once. "What did he look like?"

"Well, he never got to be premier on account of his looks," said Marilla. "Such a nose that man had! But he can speak. I was proud of being a Conservative. Rachel Lynde, being a Liberal, had no use for him. Your lunch is in the oven, Anne, and you can help yourself to some blue plum preserves out in the pantry. Matthew told me about last night. It was certainly fortunate you knew what to do because I wouldn't have."

After Anne had eaten her lunch, Marilla said that Mrs. Barry had been over to see her. "She says you saved Minny May's life, and she

She Found Marilla Knitting in the Kitchen.

is terribly sorry for the way she acted about the currant wine. She says she knows now you didn't mean to get Diana drunk, and she hopes you'll forgive her and be good friends with Diana again. You can go visit this evening, for Diana has a bad cold and can't go out."

"Oh, Marilla, can I go right now without washing my dishes? I can't think of anything so unromantic as washing dishes at this thrilling moment!"

"Yes, yes, run along," said Marilla indulgently. Then she stopped short. "Anne Shirley, come back this instant and put something on! Look at you tearing through the orchard with hair streaming. You're going to catch a death of cold."

When Anne returned to Green Gables later, she had a song in her heart. "You see before you a perfectly happy person, Marilla. Mrs. Barry had an elegant tea especially for me just as if I was real company. Nobody ever used their best china on my account before."

"Nobody Ever Used Their Best China Before."

"So you mended your fences?" Marilla asked.

"Oh, yes. Mrs. Barry kissed me and cried and said she was so sorry and that she could never repay me. I told her 'I have no hard feelings for you, Mrs. Barry. I assure you that I did not mean to intoxicate Diana, and henceforth I shall cover the past with a mantle of oblivion.' That was a pretty dignified speech, wasn't it, Marilla? And Diana and I had a wonderful afternoon together. We pledged to ask Mr. Phillips to let us sit together in school."

It wasn't long after Anne's reunion with Diana that Mr. Phillips announced he would be leaving Avonlea school in June. On his last day, all the girls were terribly upset. Even Anne came home with red eyes.

"I never knew you were so fond of Mr. Phillips," said Marilla in astonishment.

"I don't think I was crying because I was so fond of him," reflected Anne. "I just cried because all the others did. After all, Mr. Phillips

Mr. Phillips Announced He Was Leaving.

had been very mean and sarcastic to me more than once. But when he got up and made his farewell speech today and said, 'The time has come for us to part,' I felt desperately sad."

"Isn't it hard to feel desperately sad with summer vacation ahead of you?" Marilla asked.

"Oh, yes," Anne said. "Summer is such a wonderful time in Avonlea. But the highlight of the whole vacation is a special party Diana has planned the end of August at Orchard Slope. It's just for the girls in our class."

"A Wonderful Time in Avonlea"

Josie Walked the Fence.

Chapter Ten

Christmas is in the Air

Diana's party began on a high note. Everything ran smoothly until the girls went out in the garden to play a new game called "daring."

Right away, Anne dared Josie Pye to walk along the top of the board fence which enclosed the garden. To everyone's amazement Josie walked the fence as nonchalantly as if she felt the feat wasn't worth a dare. She descended from her perch flushed with victory and glared defiantly at Anne.

"So you walked a low board fence," Anne said. "I knew a girl in Marysville who could walk the ridgepole of a roof."

"I dare you to do it," Josie taunted. "I dare you to climb up and walk the ridgepole of Mr. Barry's kitchen roof."

"Don't do it, Anne," Diana begged. "You'll fall off and be killed. Never mind Josie Pye. It isn't fair to dare anybody to do anything so dangerous."

"I must do it. My honor is at stake," said Anne, turning pale. "I shall walk the ridgepole, Diana, or perish in the attempt. If I am killed, my pearl bead ring goes to you."

Anne climbed the ladder amid breathless silence, reached the ridgepole, and started to walk along it, fighting waves of dizziness. Suddenly she swayed, lost her balance, and slid down the sunbaked roof. Her friends shrieked in terror as she crashed to the ground.

If Anne had tumbled off the roof on the side where she ascended, Diana probably would have fallen heir to the pearl bead ring. Fortunately she fell on the other side where the roof

She Slid Down the Roof.

extended down over the porch so close to the ground that the fall was not a serious one.

Nevertheless, when all the girls rushed frantically around the house, they found Anne lying all white and limp in the Virginia creeper.

"Anne, are you dead?" shrieked Diana, throwing herself on her knees beside her friend. "Oh, Anne, dear Anne, say something."

To the immense relief of all the girls, especially Josie Pye, Anne sat up dizzily and answered, "No, Diana, I am not dead, but my ankle—oh, my ankle! I'm in terrible pain. Please find your father and ask him to take me home."

Marilla was in the orchard picking summer apples when she saw Mr. Barry coming over the log bridge and up the slope with Mrs. Barry beside him and a whole procession of little girls trailing after him. In his arms he carried Anne; her head lay limply against his shoulder.

"Anne, Are You Dead?"

Marilla turned white. It had been a little over a year since Anne had come to live with them. Fear stabbed suddenly at her heart. She realized that this child was dearer to her than anything else on earth.

"Mr. Barry, what has happened to Anne?" she cried, more frightened and shaken than the self-contained, sensible Marilla had been in many years.

"Don't be afraid, Marilla. I was walking the ridgepole and I fell off," Anne answered, lifting her head. "I think I may have sprained my ankle."

"I might have known you'd go and do something of the sort when I let you go to the party. Bring her in, Mr. Barry, and lay her on the sofa. Mercy me, the child has gone and fainted!"

Matthew came rushing in from the fields and raced to town to get the doctor who announced grimly after examining Anne, "I'm afraid that ankle is broken." He gave strict in-

"What Has Happened to Anne?"

structions for his patient to stay home for six to eight weeks.

At first Anne was terribly upset. This confinement meant she would miss the beginning of school and getting acquainted with the new lady teacher.

But, in the tedious weeks that followed, many friends, young and old, flocked to see her. From Mr. Bell and Josie Pye to Diana and Mrs. Allen, the new minister's wife, her visitors showered her with flowers and books and delivered news of Avonlea and school.

When at last Anne returned to school in October, she was ecstatic about her new teacher. Miss Stacy was young and sympathetic, with the ability to bring out the best in her students. Anne bloomed like a flower under her influence and carried home to the admiring Matthew and the critical Marilla glowing accounts of her school work and goals.

Of all the new projects Miss Stacy introduced, the most exciting by far was the concert

Many Friends Flocked to See Her.

to be held on Christmas night. The purpose was to raise money for the schoolhouse flag. Despite Marilla's disapproval of the event, Anne was overjoyed as she had two recitations to make.

"Oh, Marilla, I just tremble when I think of it, but it's a nice thrilly kind of tremble. Don't you hope your little Anne will distinguish herself?"

"All I hope is that you'll behave yourself. I'll be glad when all this fuss is over, and you'll be able to settle down. You are simply good for nothing just now with your head stuffed full of dialogues. It's a wonder your tongue is not clean worn out."

Anne sighed and slipped outside to where Matthew was splitting wood. Perched on a block beside him, she related every single detail regarding the Christmas recital.

"Well now, I reckon it's going to be a pretty good concert. And I expect you will say your lines just fine," Matthew said, smiling at her

She Related Every Detail.

tenderly. These two were the best of friends, but Matthew thanked his stars that he didn't have the job of raising her. That was Marilla's duty.

Yet one thing really bothered Matthew and that was the fact that Marilla dressed Anne so plainly. He first noticed just how dreary Anne's clothes were one night when she and some of her friends, all stylishly dressed, were practicing for the Christmas concert in the sitting room at Green Gables. Right then and there, he decided to give Anne a pretty dress with puffed sleeves for Christmas.

The very next day the woman-shy Matthew went to buy the dress. He deliberately chose Samuel Larson's store because he knew either Mr. Larson or his son would wait on him. To his shock, a niece of Mr. Larson's was behind the counter. Smartly dressed, she had a huge pompadour, big flirtatious brown eyes, and a dazzling smile. Matthew was so overwhelmed by her that he ordered a garden rake, hayseed,

He Went to Buy the Dress.

and finally twenty pounds of brown sugar.

"Brown sugar!" exclaimed Marilla when Matthew got home. "Whatever possessed you to get so much?"

"I guess I thought it would come in handy," said Matthew, making his escape.

Finally Matthew realized that he needed a woman to help him select a dress for Anne Since he felt Marilla would only throw cold water on the idea, he consulted Mrs. Rachel Lynde.

"Why don't I just make a dress?" Mrs. Rachel suggested. "I like sewing, and I'll make it to fit my niece, Jenny Gillis. She and Anne are as alike as two peas."

"Well now, I'm much obliged," said Matthew, "and—I dunno—but I think they make the sleeves with puffs nowadays."

"Puffs? Of course. You needn't worry a speck more about it, Matthew. I'll make it up in the very latest fashion." After he had gone, she said to herself, "Think of Matthew seeing how

Matthew Consulted Mrs. Rachel.

that poor child needed a pretty dress. Why, that man is waking up after being asleep for sixty years." On Christmas Eve, Mrs. Rachel delivered Anne's new dress to Matthew.

The next day all of Avonlea awoke to a beautiful white world. Just enough snow had fallen in the night to transform the town. Anne peered out from the frosted windows of Green Gables in delight.

"Merry Christmas, Matthew! Merry Christmas, Marilla! Isn't it a lovely white Christmas?" she cried, running downstairs. "Why, Matthew, is that for me?"

"Yes, this is my Christmas present for you," said Matthew, holding up a pale brown silk dress with two beautiful puff sleeves and rows of shirring and bows of brown silk ribbon. "Do you like it?"

"Like it! Oh, Matthew, it's perfectly exquisite," Anne said, laying the dress over a chair and clasping her hands. "Just look at those sleeves."

A Beautiful White World

"Well, well, let us eat breakfast," interrupted Marilla. "I must say, Anne, I don't think you needed that dress, but since Matthew has gotten it for you, see that you take good care of it. There's a hair ribbon Mrs. Rachel left for you. It's brown to match the dress. Come now, sit down."

"I don't see how I'm going to eat breakfast," said Anne dreamily. "Breakfast is so commonplace at such an exciting moment. I'd rather feast my eyes on that dress."

"Don't forget you have a busy day ahead of you," said Marilla. "You have to go to school and decorate the hall, and you have to have one last rehearsal before the concert tonight."

"Oh, Marilla, I'm scared," Anne cried suddenly, dropping her fork in her plate. "Suppose I forget all my lines? Suppose I open my mouth and can't speak at all?"

"Suppose I Can't Speak at All?"

Anne Was the Star.

Chapter Eleven

How Anne Got a New Hair-Do

The Christmas concert was a tremendous success. Despite Anne's stagefright, she was the star of the evening.

"Hasn't it been a wonderful night?" she sighed when it was all over, and she and Diana were walking home together under a dark, starry sky.

"I guess we must have made as much as ten dollars," Diana said. "Mr. Allan is going to send a write-up about it to the Charlottetown paper."

"Oh, Diana, will we really see our names in

print? Your solo was perfectly elegant. I was so proud of you!"

"And your recitations simply brought down the house, Anne."

"Oh, I was so nervous. I felt as if a million eyes were looking at me, and for one dreadful moment, I was sure I couldn't begin at all. Then I thought of my new puff sleeves and took courage. I knew I had to live up to those sleeves."

That night after Anne had gone to bed, Matthew and Marilla sat talking by the kitchen fire.

"Well now, I guess Anne did as well as any of them," said Matthew.

"Yes, she did," admitted Marilla. "She is a bright child. And she looked real nice, too. I was kind of opposed to this concert scheme, but I guess there's no harm in it. Anyhow, I was proud of Anne tonight, although I'm not going to tell her so."

"I did tell her so," Matthew said, "right be-

Talking by the Fire

fore she went to bed."

"She'll be thirteen in March," Marilla commented. "I suppose we should be thinking about sending her to Queen's Academy. But there's plenty of time to decide about that."

The winter weeks slipped quietly by. January turned into February, and February turned into March. Early in the month Anne celebrated her birthday with Diana.

"Just think, I'm thirteen years old today," Anne said to her best friend. "I can scarcely believe I'm in my teens. When I awoke this morning, it seemed that everything must be different. In two more years I'll be really grown-up."

In many respects Anne was already quite mature. She was a highly disciplined student who enjoyed writing compositions so much that she founded a story club. The group, composed of Diana, Ruby Gillis, Jane Andrews and Anne, met in the afternoons after school to write fiction on a regular basis.

"I'm 13 Years Old Today."

"It's extremely interesting," Anne told Marilla. "Each girl has to read her story out loud, and then we all discuss it. They all do pretty well, but I have to tell them what to write about. That isn't hard because I have millions of ideas."

"Such foolishness," scoffed Marilla. "You're wasting time you should be spending on your lessons."

"But we're careful to put a moral in each story," explained Anne. "All the good people are rewarded and all the bad ones are punished. I do try to be a good person myself, but it's so hard. I hope to be like Mrs. Allan when I grow up. Do you think there is a chance of that, Marilla?"

"I shouldn't say there was a great deal," Marilla snapped. "I'm sure Mrs. Allan was never such a silly, forgetful girl as you are."

"No, but she wasn't always as good as she is now either," Anne said seriously. "She told me herself that she was very mischievous when

"Such Foolishness."

she was a girl and was always getting into scrapes."

Like every teen-age girl growing up, Anne continued to get into her share of scrapes, too. Late one afternoon in April, Marilla returned home from a meeting of the Ladies' Aid Society expecting to find Anne at work in the kitchen and the table all set for dinner. To her dismay, the fire was out and Anne was nowhere in sight.

"That girl is gadding about somewhere with Diana, writing stories or some other tomfoolery and forgetting all about her duties," Marilla complained to Matthew who had just come in from plowing. "I must say I've never known Anne to be untrustworthy before."

"Well now, I dunno," said Matthew. "Don't call her untrustworthy until you're sure she's disobeyed you. Mebbe it can all be explained."

Marilla prepared supper, washed and dried the dishes all in grim silence. Still there was no sign of Anne.

"That Girl Is Gadding About Somewhere."

In search of a candle to light the cellar, Marilla went up to Anne's room. When she lit the candle on the bedside table, she saw Anne lying facedown in the pillows.

"Mercy on us," cried the astonished Marilla. "Have you been asleep, Anne?"

"No, and I'm not sick either. Please go away, Marilla, and don't look at me."

"Anne Shirley, what is the matter with you? Get up this minute and tell me."

"Look at my hair," Anne whispered.

"Why, it's green!" cried Marilla, looking at Anne's hair, flowing in heavy masses down her back.

"Yes, it's green," moaned the distraught girl. "I thought nothing could be as bad as red hair. But this is ten times worse. I'm sorry now that I dyed it."

"Dyed it! Dyed your hair? Well," said Marilla sarcastically, "if I were going to dye my hair, I wouldn't have dyed it green."

"But I didn't mean to dye it green," Anne ex-

"Don't Look at Me."

plained. "I bought this dye from a peddler who promised me my hair would be a raven black. He swore the color would not wash out."

Time proved that the peddler was right on one point. The color was permanent. Despite the fact Anne hid away at home for a week and washed and scrubbed her hair every day, the color remained a ghastly yellow-green.

"It's no use, Anne. That is fast dye if there ever was any," Marilla said one afternoon. "Your hair must be cut off; there is no other way."

"All right. Just do it and get it over with, Marilla," Anne pleaded.

Picking up her scissors, Marilla shingled Anne's hair as closely to her head as possible. The mortified teen-ager looked in the mirror once, screamed and swore she'd never look again.

Anne's clipped head created a sensation at school when she returned. To her relief no one guessed she had dyed her hair green—not

Picking Up Her Scissors

even Josie Pye who told her she looked like a perfect scarecrow.

"Diana says that when my hair begins to grow, I should wear a black velvet ribbon around my head with a bow on the side," Anne told Marilla, who was lying on the sofa late one afternoon nursing one of her headaches. "She thinks it will be very becoming."

Fortunately Anne's hair grew rapidly. As it grew in, it formed soft, silky curls all over her head. As Diana had suggested, Anne wore a black velvet ribbon to keep it in place.

"Your hair is real pretty now. I'd say it has turned a true auburn," Diana said to Anne one day when the story club met at the pond at Orchard Slope to act out Tennyson's poem "Elaine", which they had learned in school. "You get my vote to play the beautiful lily maid, Elaine."

Ruby Gillis and Jane Andrews both agreed. Thrilled to be cast as the lead character, Anne threw a faded piano shawl around her neck

Anne's Hair Grew Rapidly.

and leaped into an old rowboat. Immediately her companions pushed the craft into the current in the direction of the bridge. Then, they went flying through the woods to meet her on the other side of the bridge.

To her horror, Anne looked down and saw that water was rushing into the boat through a hole in the bottom. She remembered the oars had been left behind on the landing. Luckily, the boat floated close to the bridge. She jumped out onto a tree trunk pile and held on as tightly as she could.

As Anne watched the rowboat sink beneath the murky water, she called out to her friends. But no one heard her, and no one came to her rescue.

Water Was Rushing In.

They Charged Through the Woods.

Chapter Twelve

The Dream of a Lifetime

Diana, Ruby and Jane had seen the rowboat sink and assumed that Anne was in it. Screaming in terror, they charged through the woods to get help—never once glancing in the direction of the bridge.

Anne's imagination ran wild. Suppose nobody ever came! Suppose she grew so tired and cramped that she could hold on no longer! She looked down into the wicked green depths below her, wavering with oily shadows, and shivered.

Then, just as she thought she could not endure the pain in her arms and wrists one more moment, a little dory appeared from under the bridge. At the the helm was none other than Gilbert Blythe!

"Anne Shirley! How on earth did you get there?" he exclaimed, looking up into her big, frightened but scornful eyes.

Without waiting for an answer, he pulled close to the pile and extended his hand. Clinging to him, Anne scrambled down into the dory where she sat embarrassed and furious in her dripping wet shawl.

"What happened, Anne?" asked Gilbert, taking up the oars.

"We were playing 'Elaine'", explained Anne, "and I had to drift down to Camelot in the barge—I mean, the rowboat. It began to leak, and I climbed out on the pile. I don't know where my friends went. Now will you be kind enough to row me to the landing?"

Gilbert rowed to the landing and got out to help Anne off. "Look here," he said suddenly,

Anne Scrambled into the Dory.

"Can't we be friends? I'm awfully sorry I made fun of your hair in school that time. It was such a long time ago. Besides I think your hair is very pretty now. What do you say?"

At first Anne's heart gave a quick little beat. But then she remembered vividly how Gilbert had humiliated her before the whole school. "No," she said coldly. "I will never be friends with you—not ever."

"All right!" Gilbert said, springing into his boat angrily. "You can be sure I'll never ask you again."

Gilbert had barely rowed away than Diana and Jane came rushing up, relieved to see their lily maid alive and in one piece.

"Oh, Anne, there was no one home at Orchard Slope or Green Gables to help us," Diana cried. "Thank heaven you're all right!"

"How did you escape?" Jane wanted to know.

"I climbed up on one of the piles," explained Anne wearily. "Gilbert Blythe came along in a dory and brought me to shore."

"I Will Never Be Friends—Not Ever."

"Oh, Anne, how romantic," cried Jane. "Of course you'll speak to him after this."

"No, I won't," retorted Anne, "and I don't want to hear the word romantic again, Jane Andrews. This experience has cured me forever of being a romantic."

Marilla was terribly annoyed with Anne over this latest escapade and scolded her soundly. The truth was she had grown to love this slim, gray-eyed girl more than life itself. The strength of her love frightened her, and as a result she hid her feelings.

Unfortunately, Anne had no idea how much Marilla adored her. For the most part she viewed her new mother as someone hard to please and totally lacking in sympathy and understanding.

Therefore, Anne was very surprised when Marilla talked to her one day that fall about studying for the entrance exam to Queen's Teaching Academy.

"Miss Stacy came over to talk to Matthew

"How Romantic!"

and me about it today," Marilla explained. "She wants to organize a class of her advanced students and give them extra lessons after school. Would you like to go to Queen's, Anne?"

"Oh, Marilla," Anne cried, "it's the dream of my lifetime to be a teacher. But isn't it terribly expensive?"

"You needn't worry about that part of it. Matthew and I want you to have a good education and be in a position to support yourself. You'll always have a home at Green Gables as long as we are alive, but this is an uncertain world. So you can join the Queen's class if you like. You will have a year and a half to prepare for the entrance exams."

And so it was that the Queen's class was organized. Gilbert Blythe, Anne Shirley, Ruby Gillis, Jane Andrews, Josie Pye, Charlie Sloane, and Moody Spurgeon MacPherson all joined. Diana Barry did not, a situation which made Anne very sad.

From the beginning Anne and Gilbert were

"The Dream of My Lifetime."

the leaders of the class. The tremendous rivalry between them increased, but beyond that Gilbert completely ignored Anne. Suddenly she discovered that it wasn't pleasant to be ignored. She also realized that somewhere along the line she *had* forgiven Gilbert. "Too bad it was too late," she thought.

Otherwise the school year passed along in a round of pleasant duties and studies. Anne was happy, eager and interested. There were lessons to be learned and honors to be won, delightful books to read, new pieces to be practiced for the Sunday School choir, and pleasant Saturday afternoons to be spent with Mrs. Allan at the manse.

In the spring a rumor circulated that Miss Stacy had been offered a teaching position in her own home district. When the Queen's class asked her about it, she told them that she was much too interested in them to even think of leaving Avonlea.

"I'm so glad," said Anne with shining eyes.

With Mrs. Allan at the Manse

"Dear Miss Stacy, it would be perfectly dreadful if you didn't come back. I don't believe I would have the heart to go on with my studies if another teacher came here."

When school opened in the fall the Queen's class knew they had to study hard in order to pass the entrance examinations which were not far off now. Anne had bad dreams where she found herself staring miserably at pass lists where Gilbert's name was blazoned at the top and hers did not appear at all.

Despite the pressure the entrance exams posed, the school year was interesting and the days just seemed to fly by. This was due largely to Miss Stacy's careful guidance. She led her class to think and explore and discover for themselves to a degree that quite shocked Mrs. Rachel Lynde and the school trustees who were highly suspicious of any new methods of teaching.

That winter Anne shot up in height so rapidly that Marilla was astonished one day, when

The Days Flew By.

they were standing side by side, to find the girl was taller than herself.

"Why Anne, how you've grown," she said. The child she had learned to love had vanished and in her place was a tall, serious young girl of fifteen. Marilla knew she would miss her terribly if she went away to school next year.

As the time to take the exams drew near, Marilla could see that Anne was worried. "How do you think you'll do?" she asked her.

"Sometimes I think I'll do all right—and then I get horribly afraid. We've studied hard and Miss Stacy has drilled us thoroughly. Oh, it would be a disgrace if I fail, especially if Gil—I mean if the others passed."

But Anne also wanted to do well for the sake of Marilla and Matthew who had done so much for her. In June the class spent a long, hard week in Charlottetown taking the entrance exams at the Academy. Competition was keen as there were students from all over Prince Edward Island.

"How You've Grown."

When it was all over, Anne thought she did well in everything but geometry. Her main hope was that she would pass and come out ahead of Gilbert. Unfortunately the pass list was not to be announced for two weeks. "How am I *ever* going to stand the suspense?" she wondered.

Anne Thought She Did Well

Shaking Hands and Sinking Feelings

Chapter Thirteen

An Ending and a Beginning

After two weeks Anne, Jane, Ruby, and Josie began haunting the post office and opening the Charlottetown paper with shaking hands and cold, sinking feelings as bad as any they had experienced during entrance week.

When three weeks had slipped by without the pass list appearing, Anne began to feel she couldn't stand the strain much longer. Her appetite failed, and she lost all interest in Avonlea doings. Noting how dejected she was every afternoon when she dragged home from the post office, Matthew couldn't help but worry about her.

Then one evening the news came. Anne was sitting at the open window of her bedroom, drinking in the beauty of the summer dusk. Suddenly she spotted Diana flying down through the firs, over the log bridge, and up the slope, with a fluttering newspaper in her hand.

"Anne, you passed!" cried Diana, dashing into her room a few minutes later. "You and Gilbert tied for first place, but your name is first on the list—first on a list of two hundred. Everyone else in the class here passed, too. Father just brought home the paper not ten minutes ago."

"I never dreamed of this," said Anne, picking up the newspaper. "Yes, I did too, just once. But it seemed so vain and presumptuous to think I could lead Prince Edward Island. Oh, Di, I must go tell Matthew."

The two girls hurried to the field below the barn where Matthew was raking hay. As luck

"Anne, You Passed!" Cried Diana.

would have it, Mrs. Rachel and Marilla were chatting at the lane fence.

"Matthew," cried Anne. "I passed. I came in first!"

"Well now, I always said it," said Matthew, gazing at the pass list in delight.

"You've done pretty well, I must say, Anne," beamed Marilla, trying to hide her pride in Anne from her critical friend.

"I guess she has done well, and far be it for me not to say so," said Mrs. Rachel generously. "You're a credit to your friends, young lady, and we're all proud of you."

After the news of Anne's acceptance to Queen's, the Cuthberts put all their energy into getting her ready to leave that fall. Anne's wardrobe for college was not only ample, but all the new clothes were stylish and pretty. Matthew saw to that.

"This green dress is perfectly lovely," said Anne one night as she modeled a frilly silk party dress for Matthew and Marilla in the

"I Came in First!"

kitchen. The gown was a special gift from Marilla, who had it custom made for evening events.

"It's the perfect thing to wear if you're asked to recite poetry at any concerts at Queen's," Marilla said. "I'm sure you will be because you have made quite a name for yourself around the Island. Who could ever forget the night you recited "The Maiden's Vow" to that packed audience in Charlottetown? My, there seems to be no end to our being proud of you!"

"Why, Marilla, I think you're crying," said Anne, kissing her tenderly. "Are you upset because I'm going away? I shall always be your own little Anne who will love you and Matthew more and better every day of her life!"

Fighting the tears himself, Matthew got up quickly and hurried outside where he sat under a poplar tree and remembered the sad, frightened orphan girl he had brought to Green Gables four years before and how she had changed their lives

"Are You Upset Because I'm Going Away?"

"Well now, I guess my putting my oar in occasionally never did any harm," he thought. "She's smart and pretty and loving, too. She's been a blessing to us, and there never was a luckier mistake than the one Mrs. Spencer made. It was Providence that brought Anne to us. The Almighty saw how much we needed her."

The September day finally arrived when Anne said good-bye to a tearful Diana and a solemn Marilla and set off with Matthew to officially enter Queen's in Charlottetown.

The first day at the Academy passed pleasantly enough in a whirl of excitement. Anne was busy meeting all the new students, learning to recognize professors, and signing up for classes.

Both Anne and Gilbert registered for Second Year work as Miss Stacy had suggested. This meant getting a First Class teacher's license in one year instead of two. It also meant a harder work load. Jane, Ruby, Josie, Charlie,

There Never Was a Luckier Mistake.

and Moody all signed up to take the Second Class work.

Consequently, Anne found herself to be a stranger in a class of fifty students. The only person she knew was her old rival, Gilbert. "My, he looks determined," she thought. "I suppose he's already made up his mind to win the medal."

Homesickness struck Anne at night when she was alone in her room at the boarding house. Although Josie Pye had never been a favorite of hers, Anne was glad to see her when she dropped by unexpectedly.

"You've been crying," remarked Josie, staring at Anne's red eyes. "I guess you're homesick. So many people have so little self-control in that respect. I have no intention of being homesick. This town is much more fun than that pokey old Avonlea. Oh, did you hear that Queen's is going to offer one of the Avery scholarships? The Board of Governors will announce it tomorrow."

The Only Person She Knew Was Gilbert.

Before Josie told her the news, Anne had been aspiring for a teacher's license, First Class, at the end of the year and perhaps the medal. But now in one moment she had a new dream—winning the Avery scholarship, enabling her to take a four year arts course at Redmond College, and receiving her B. A. degree.

The scholarship, which paid two hundred fifty dollars a year for four years, would be awarded to the June graduate with the highest marks in English and English literature. While these were Anne's best subjects, she knew she would have to work harder than ever before to win.

Anne's homesickness wore off largely because of weekend visits home. As long as the good weather lasted, the Avonlea students took the train home every Friday night. Diana and other old friends were always there to greet them, catch up on their news, and walk them to their houses.

She Had a New Dream.

However, after the Christmas holidays the Avonlea crowd stayed on campus on weekends and buckled down to work. Certain facts had been generally accepted. The medal contestants had been narrowed down to three—Gilbert, Anne, and Lewis Wilson. Of the six students who were considered to be in the running for the Avery scholarship, a girl named Emily Clay was thought to be the top candidate.

Night after night during the long winter, Anne stayed up into the wee hours pouring over her lessons and laboring over her compositions. Still she didn't have high hopes of winning the scholarship because Emily Clay always spoke up so brilliantly in class and continued to get high marks.

Then almost before anybody knew it, spring had come to Charlottetown. Unfortunately all the harassed students thought or talked about were their upcoming exams. For Anne, exam week was a grueling ordeal. She was glad

Night After Night of the Long Winter

when it was over.

On the morning when the final results of the exams were posted, Anne and Jane walked together to the administration building at Queen's.

"I have no hope of winning the Avery," Anne said as they walked in the door, "but the medal is certainly a possibility. Oh, I don't have the courage to go look at the bulletin board in front of everyone and see who won. Promise me you will go do it for me."

It turned out that that wasn't necessary. The hall was full of boys who were carrying Gilbert on their shoulders and yelling at the top of their lungs, "Hurrah for Blythe, medalist!"

Pale and shaken, Anne felt the sickening pangs of defeat and heartbreak. She had failed; Gilbert had won. And Matthew had been so sure she would win the medal.

The Hall Was Full of Boys.

"Winner of the Avery!"

Chapter Fourteen

The Bend in the Road

As Anne and Jane started to walk out of the building, somebody suddenly cried, "Three cheers for Anne Shirley, winner of the Avery!"

Excited friends surrounded the two girls, congratulating Anne enthusiastically. Her shoulders were squeezed and her hands shaken over and over. Throughout it all, she managed to whisper to Jane, "Won't Matthew and Marilla be pleased? I must write to them right away!" Tears of joy filled her eyes.

Commencement, the next important happening, was held in the assembly hall at the

Academy. Addresses were given, essays read, songs sung, and the public award of diplomas, prizes and medals made.

Matthew and Marilla were there, with eyes for only one student on the platform, a tall girl in pale green, who read the best essay and was named the winner of the prized Avery scholarship.

"Reckon you're glad we kept her, Marilla?" whispered Matthew, nudging his sister.

"Stuff and nonsense. It's not the first time I've been glad," Marilla snapped back.

Anne went home to Avonlea with her family that evening. She had not been at Green Gables since April and was thrilled to see Diana again.

The next morning at breakfast it suddenly struck Anne that Matthew was not looking well. Marilla confirmed Anne's suspicions and admitted that Matthew had had some bad spells with his heart that spring.

She also confessed that her headaches were

A Tall Girl in Pale Green

occurring more frequently and that her new glasses had not done any good. However, she promised Anne she would consult a well-known oculist who was coming to the Island soon.

In early evening Anne went with Matthew to bring in the cows. He walked slowly back through the woods with his head bent. Anne walked in step with him, drinking in the beautiful sunset.

"You've been working too hard lately, Matthew," she chided him. "Why don't you take life easier?"

"Well now, I can't seem to," said Matthew, as he opened the gate to let the cows through. "Guess I'm just used to working hard."

"If I had been the boy you sent for," said Anne wistfully, "I'd be able to help you now."

"I'd rather have you than a dozen boys, Anne," said Matthew, patting her hand. "After all, it wasn't a boy who won the Avery scholarship. It was my girl—my girl who I'm so

Drinking in the Beautiful Sunset

proud of."

He smiled his shy smile at her and went in the yard. Anne took the memory of that moment with her when she went to her room that night. She sat for a long time thinking of the past and dreaming of the future.

The next morning as she came through the front hall, her hands full of narcissi, she heard Marilla cry out, "Matthew—Matthew—what's the matter? Are you sick?"

Matthew, his face drawn and gray, staggered back and forth in the porch doorway, a folded newspaper in his hand. Anne and Marilla rushed to his side, but before they could reach him, he collapsed.

"He's fainted," gasped Marilla. "Anne, run for Martin. Quick! He's at the barn."

Martin, the hired man, started at once for the doctor, calling at Orchard Slope on his way to send Mr. and Mrs. Barry over. Mrs. Rachel, who was there visiting, came too. They found Anne and Marilla desperately trying to revive

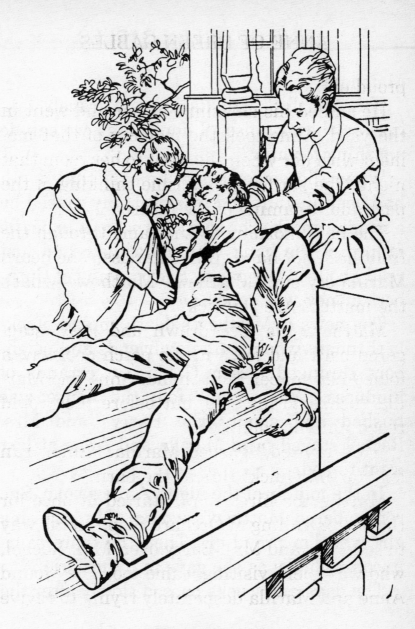

He Collapsed.

Matthew.

"Oh, Marilla," Mrs. Rachel said gravely, taking Matthew's pulse. "I don't think we can do anything for him."

When the doctor came, he said that death had been instant and was probably caused by a sudden shock. The shock turned out to be the failure of the bank which Matthew had just read about in the paper. Every penny of Cuthbert money was gone.

The news of Matthew's death spread quickly through Avonlea. All day friends and neighbors thronged Green Gables on errands of kindness. When night fell, the house was hushed and silent. The Barrys and Mrs. Rachel stayed until Marilla and Anne at last went to bed.

In the middle of the night, Anne awoke. She remembered Matthew's words, "My girl—my girl who I'm proud of." Then the tears came uncontrollably, as she gave in to her grief.

The days and weeks passed slowly after the

Every Penny Was Gone.

funeral. Anne planted a white rosebush at Matthew's grave and went there often to tend the plot.

One afternoon when she returned home, she found Marilla sitting very dejectedly in the kitchen. "Are you tired?" Anne asked.

"It's not that. I saw the eye doctor today. He says that if I give up nearly all my activities and wear new glasses, my eyes may not get worse. Otherwise I'll be stone blind in six months."

"Marilla, you mustn't think the worst," Anne said, stunned. "The doctor has given you hope."

I don't call it much hope," said Marilla bitterly. "What is there to live for if I can't use my eyes? I think I'm going to have to sell the farm and board somewhere—maybe with Rachel. Thank heaven you have that scholarship."

"You can't sell Green Gables," Anne cried, her mind whirling. "I won't let you lose your home!"

A White Rosebush

"I wish I didn't have to," Marilla lamented, "but you can see I can't live here alone. And eventually my eyesight will go."

"You won't have to stay here by yourself. I'll live with you. I'm not going to Redmond," Anne declared.

"Not going to Redmond? What do you mean?"

"Just what I say. Marilla, surely you don't think I would leave you alone in your trouble after all you've done for me? I'm sure Mr. Barry will rent the farm, and I can teach either in Avonlea or Carmody. I'll keep you cheered up and we'll be cozy and happy together."

"Oh, Anne, it sounds wonderful. But I can't let you sacrifice your dream of college for me."

"It's no sacrifice. I can study college courses right here at home. The worst thing we could possibly do is to give up Green Gables. I'm sixteen and a half now, and my mind is made up."

"You blessed girl!" said Marilla, throwing

"Not Going to Redmond?"

her arms around Anne, "you have given me new life. I love you for it, but then I've always loved you. I just was never able to say it before." Anne quickly returned the hug, and they both cried a little.

When it became known around Avonlea that Anne Shirley had given up the idea of going to college and intended to stay home and teach, there was a lot of talk about it. Most of the good folks, not knowing about Marilla's eyes, thought Anne was foolish. However, Mrs. Allan told her she had done a wonderful thing.

Mrs. Rachel also had plenty to say. "Well, Anne, I was glad to hear you have given up your notion of going to college. You've got as much education as a woman can be comfortable with."

In the next breath she informed Anne that the trustees had given her the post at Avonlea school. Apparently Gilbert had submitted his application but withdrawn it when he heard about Anne's situation. He planned to teach at

The Trustees Had Given Her the Post.

White Sands.

Deeply touched by Gilbert's sacrifice, Anne stopped by the Blythe home to thank him. "It was very good of you to give up so much for me. I really appreciate it."

"I was glad I was able to do you some small service, Anne. I hope this means we can forget the past and be good friends."

"Gil, I've been a silly goose. I hope you can forgive me."

"We are going to be the best of friends," said Gil jubilantly. "We were born to be good friends, Anne. You've thwarted destiny long enough. I know we can help each other in many ways. You are going to keep up your studies, aren't you? So am I. Come, I'm going to walk home with you."

Gilbert and Anne walked slowly back to Green Gables, pausing at the gate and talking on and on as if to make up for lost time.

When he left, Anne stood at the gate thinking "When I left Queen's, my future stretched

"I've Been a Silly Goose."

before me like a straight road. Now there's a bend in it. I don't know what lies around the bend, but I believe in my dreams and ideals. Nothing can take those from me. God's in his heaven; all's right in the world."

She went slowly inside.

"I Believe in My Dreams."